CB Barrie

Good Vibrations

Éditions
DÉDICACES

First published by Editions Dedicaces in 2016.

ISBN: 978-1-77076-618-1

This book was professionally typeset on Reedsy.
Find out more at reedsy.com

Contents

Prologue

Christ! What a bloody mess!

He stared utterly mortified and despairing at the scene that confronted him.

Now, at three a.m. on a cold forlorn morning, and like three previous mournful pre-dawn occasions, he looked through the windscreen of his car surveying the wreckage of his business, and the potential wreckage of his life. His nationally renowned shop, and consequently his whole livelihood, had been the victim of yet another raid - this time a ram raid.

The night sky glowed an orange white as the sodium streetlights and the police floodlights competed to illuminate the devastation of the two shattered shop fronts, thereby allowing a few uniformed men to carefully pick their way through all the rubble, debris and detritus that the ram raiders had dispensed.

Two gaping black holes, that now marked his two shop windows, stood out in the long line of shop fronts like two rotten teeth in a row of otherwise gleaming dental perfection. Four police cars blocked the high street, two pointing uptown and the other two down. In between, a fire appliance was parked opposite the premises and three firemen were attempting to sweep the remains of his two extensive shop windows off the road and into piles. Two others shovelled the shards and fragments into two plastic wheelie-bins.

What was left of the two meshed steel security shutters had been pulled away from the gaping hollow where his shop displays had been and were now marooned upright against a nearside wall. Neither resembled their original form; they stood twisted and mangled, hit by so enormous a force that they had been torn from their supports and buckled into misshapen scrap. Their distorted shape, one locked inside the other and nestling up against the vertical masonry, made it appear as though two huge spider webs were stretching themselves across the brickwork.

He halted his car, nosing it as close to the two blocking police cruisers as he could get, noting that even this far from the shop he could see the crushed remains of two high grade audio amplifiers laying forlornly in the gutter.

The remains of the amplifiers foretold everything he was to find that night – the utter loss of his best stock, the major damage to his premises, not to mention the suspension of business while everything was renewed.

Worst of all, he had yet another battle on his hands to find any insurance. Even if the present policy was invoked and paid out, he knew full well that the cover would not be continued; they had warned him of that after the third break in. In short, he was now virtually uninsurable and were it possible to arrange insurance, the premiums would be exorbitant and subject to impossibly stringent restrictions and conditions. He didn't believe in miracles or fairy tales and his stomach dropped as he realised that short of divine intervention, he was facing a very steep uphill struggle to avoid the loss of everything he had so painstakingly built up.

When the call came from the police so early in the morning he was at first too tired to respond. Instead Carol, his long-suffering wife, had taken the call but the caller had insisted that he, as the key holder of the premises, be spoken to. However, it made no difference, she knew immediately why they had called and was already in tears as he picked up the receiver.

He recognised the voice at the other end. Sergeant Neilson had been the source of bad tidings on previous occasions and this time his voice conveyed some genuine sympathy.

"Sorry to be the messenger of dire news – the bastards have hit your shop again...you need to get here asap."

And so he did, not caring about the speed limits and taking the view that being pulled over for a speeding offence would simply be black icing on one enormous pile of misfortune.

As it happened, on his way into town he saw not a trace of the police, which given the circumstances didn't surprise him. No doubt they were either all in town, uselessly surrounding his shop, or out on the bypass making some poor motorist's life hell for a niggling traffic offence. The chances of them actually being in pursuit of the villains who had nailed his shop were lower than the chances of winning the lottery.

Not once had the police even hinted at being close to arresting anyone for all the three previous successful break-ins. Not even a sniff of being able to identify the robbers, or of tracing the tens of thousands worth of products that had vanished like a magicians best trick. 'No forensic trail' the useless CID had tiredly repeated to him after each query about progress – no indication whatsoever of what had become of the felons or his precious stock. It was almost as if they blamed him for running a business so attractive to thieves. One of the junior detectives even admitted that his business was an irresistible temptation to the professional bandits – because he traded in the hi-fi equivalent of a Porsche dealership. What he sold was top end audio and like the expensive Porches, Mercedes and BMW's, the crooks would plunder to order.

As he exited his car, Sergeant Neilson, the legs of his uniform peppered and streaked with powdered plaster, came out of one of the gutted shop fronts, and on seeing his arrival walked up to him.

"Hello Mr. Lincoln, hell of a mess I'm afraid. When the alarms triggered, they only operated for about ten seconds – somehow the gang defeated the electronics before the false-alarm time-out period ended, so no silent warning got sent to the police station. It was only because a newspaper delivery van saw the raiders wagon pull out of the second shop front that we came to know about it. He got a 999 call in, but stayed too far back to identify the people involved. It seems you and I have been through this disaster once too often. I can only sympathise with you and tell you we will do all we can to catch the shits that did this."

He stood where he had arrived with Neilson standing by his side, only listening with half an ear to what the Sergeant was saying. It was as the final expression of commiserations came out from the policeman that he felt the upsurge of resentment and fury at all the ineffectual and pointless support the law had provided.

"What about the bloody street cameras – the CCTV...surely something was picked up?"

Neilson shrugged, "We don't know yet. There is no one manning the surveillance desk at the moment so we will have to rely on what's been recorded – if anything. That said, don't get your hopes up, we think the gang would be masked and all we are likely to get from the video is the kind of wagon they used. You can be sure they'll transfer your stuff to another vehicle...and soon the wagon they used to trash your shop will either disappear into a breakers yard or be abandoned and burnt to ashes somewhere in the middle of nowhere."

He nodded his head, incapable of offering anything useful in reply.

"I'll just go and look, I need to...."

Neilson stood aside as he stepped forward in the direction of his gutted premises, desperate to see the full extent of his vile luck.

He walked through one of the shattered holes that had once displayed his pride and joy, a featured range of top quality sound reproduction equipment – the side of his shop that had housed every famous name in audio electronics. The other side of the shop retailed guitar amplifiers, guitar sound modifiers, public address systems, microphones, cabling, echo chambers and so on for rock bands and the like, but even that had been pillaged.

His feet crunched on broken masonry, brick rubble, crushed plasterwork and some smaller shards of window glass; even the low front walls that had supported the massive display windows had been smashed by whatever powerful machine the raiders had used to break through. He looked around at what was left; the outside police floodlights combining with the streetlights filtered in, illuminating an eerie scene of utter devastation. Almost everything had been taken or destroyed in the raiders greed to get at what they wanted. His foot caught something heavy and as he looked down at his feet he saw the mangled chassis of a *Thermio Tec* stereo power amplifier surrounded by the trampled remains of its twelve glass encased thermionic valves. Fragments of the control panel lay about and a few remains of the silver control knobs glittered in the uneven light. Even the stand the amplifier had stood on lay twisted, broken and trampled into the ground. It had once taken centre stage in the window display. It broke his heart – a bespoke amplifier retailing at over £4000, and the idiots had simply run over it.

As his eyes searched further into the recesses of the shop, he tried to remember where everything had been and what was missing. He was far too tired and dispirited and there was too much destruction to give him a clear picture, but it was obvious the raiders had known exactly what they intended to take and what they could leave. Some of the shelves and a few display stands were partially intact. Though displaced by the frenzied work of the raiders, a few second level *Naylor & Crossly* power amplifiers and three *Marden* pre-amplifiers had been left behind. Two prized pristine *Garrard 301* record decks with 12 inch *SME* transcription arms were the forlorn remnants of the section displaying vintage high end transcription vinyl record turntables; everything else, particularly the modern studio standard units and top of the range CD players had vanished. Yet, at the back of the shop, now white with dust and debris, the bigger but heavy *Tannoy* and *B&W* speaker units had been omitted from their swag. Even the vintage *Quad 22* and *Quad 33* amplifiers and sixties era FM tuners had been ignored.

There was no doubt, whatever their criminal thinking, the bastards were well organised. As best he could judge, and looking over the residue of the *Marshall, Vox* and *Selmer* guitar amplifier section of his business, they knew exactly what they should acquire to maximise their takings and minimise the effort.

He could more or less calculate their haul; the value of all the high-grade amps, and everything else, would amount to some £280,000. Add the repairs to the shop, the interim costs while the shop was closed and the organising of a full restock, it was going to exceed £550,000 – and it would take one hell of a fight to get it sorted!

1

He arrived home distraught, sick at heart and utterly shattered.

The early morning sunlight was just beginning to glow into radiance in the morning mist, with the light bleeding outwards from the sun's diffused halo. It was going to be a fine day, but he had no interest in seeing it, it simply heralded the forthcoming months of hassle and disappointment he would be forced to endure.

Before he left, the police had cordoned off the two shop fronts and had agreed to arrange for boarding to be put up to seal the open access to the interior. He'd been advised by an unusually sympathetic police detective to contact his insurance agents immediately so that they could see the full extent of the damage before the police forensic teams started work. He almost laughed, there was no difference between totally gutted premises and totally devastated premises subsequently picked clean for any evidence – in every respect the whole damn thing was a write off. His insurance agent would take his own sweet time getting the loss adjustors and loss of earnings appraisers in – and why not? There was no commission for his agent in settling a substantial claim.

Prior experience told him that the insurers would procrastinate for as long as possible before settling. They would grudgingly forward a cheque that was likely post dated three months and then omit an authorising signature. Just as on a previous occasion, it would be an exercise in delaying the payout, fatuously excused as an administrative error!

The house greeted him as though it was waiting for bad news – an oppressive hush seemingly pervaded the whole interior as he closed the front door. He called out, but his voice drowned in the forbidding silence.

Upstairs he found Carol asleep in her dressing gown on top of their bed. She had stayed behind in the house after the police call and worried herself to sleep. She seemed to slumber fitfully, her closed eyes still red and swollen from her weeping. It had been worse for her; she had no one to call on for help, no one to turn to while he was away. He knew how she saw herself; as self-reliant and considerate – even to the point of being unnecessarily stoic. Her friends were not to be woken at three a.m. in the morning with bad news, nor with her entreating them for help. She would keep it to herself; carrying and containing the burden of all the misfortune as though it might contaminate those close to her. Yet he knew also the extent of her insecurities. Ever since their first two children had died after only a few months of life, she had clung to him for reassurance and comfort, as though she feared even he would be taken away from her.

In truth, Carol had very little enduring resilience and she needed all his attention to be certain she was worthy and valued. He realised that she carried a deep sense of guilt, as though it was her fault that she had borne two sickly children and failed to give her husband the heir he deserved.

He'd never really convinced her that he felt no blame towards her, that he was simply grateful that she was still his, and that

2

she had survived the births. He'd always wanted her to sincerely believe that he thanked God every day that she was there waiting for him when he got home.

Looking at the love of his life he too felt a surge of guilt as he realised how often she had gone through the trauma she had experienced again tonight.

What was he to say? How was he going to persuade her that for the moment at least nothing would change. That they had enough reserves to pay the bills for a while and there was no need to think they would immediately go under. He would ensure she would not want for anything, and that no matter how difficult it became he would never give up in his intention to rebuild everything.

And yet he knew it was going to be difficult, she would see disaster in every setback, and many setbacks there would be. But he was going to restore all that had been lost, of that he was determined. His one hope was that Carol would survive the restoration with her sanity intact.

As he gazed at his wife, almost succumbing to the waves of tiredness that beset him, his mind ran over all the immediate consequences of the raiders work he had recently left behind. He knew that regardless of his exhausted state he was obliged to get word to his staff, to stop them readying themselves for the mornings attendance in the shop – they would not automatically and instantly find out there was now no shop to go to.

It was imperative to reassure them that as soon as possible he would continue as before. However, in the meantime he had no choice but to suspend them on half pay, hoping that they would remain loyal to him as the shop rebuild was enacted. He needed Mark Stapleford, his electronic repairs manager, to handle everything – he was at the limit of his endurance and was in no fit state to handle the tide of emotion he knew all the phone calls to his staff would elicit. Mark's was the one phone call he had to make - and the one phone call he dreaded having to make. Doubtless, Mark would find it no easier in turn.

As he dialled Mark's number using his bedside phone he heard Carol stir and then saw her shudder. Deciding it would be better not to disturb her, he replaced the receiver and made his way downstairs to the hallway phone but then, realising how dry, debilitated and weary he was, his next thought was to make a coffee before phoning Mark.

As he waited in the kitchen for the kettle to boil he ran over the things that he needed to do to begin the recovery. It wasn't just getting the insurers to agree compensation and for the refurbishment work on the shops to start, he had to re-stock, and re-stock with the same range of top equipment he had built his reputation on. But that would, or could be, very problematic. Some of the hi-fi brands he stocked were hand built and slow to arrive, others were rare imported items. Some were famous systems targeted by single-minded audiophiles who would accept nothing less than a perfect example of an audio amplifier made decades before. It had taken him years of careful hunting to become the country's primary source of classic and vintage amplifiers. In short, he had a lot of hard work to get through in order to stock what amounted to a unique range of equipment. Mark would help, so too some of his trade contacts. With luck he could eventually restore the status quo.

Sipping his coffee he listened to the dialling tone reach out to its number, then heard it being replaced by a "Hello, Mark Stapleford."

"Mark, this is Edmund, I have some really bad news. The shop was ram-raided early this morning and it's a disaster. I want you to go over there as soon as you can and salvage everything worth retaining. Before that please..."

There was a gasp of dismay at the end of the line as he began his instructions. Knowing that the news had hit Mark as hard as it had hit him, he hesitated.

"Yeah, sorry Mark but there was no easy way to tell you. Now don't worry for yourself, I will guarantee your salary for the interim so you and Fiona will be safe. However, I can only afford half pay for the rest of the team until the insurance people decide to settle. Now, please phone everyone else on staff and tell them what I have told you – they keep their jobs; half pay until we restart – that is if they are willing – and we will try to get back to trading again as soon as everything else is resolved. That said Mark, you will have to excuse me. I've been up since three, I've had a bloody horrible time and I'm fit for fuck all at the moment. Give me a day to recover a bit and we will get together to formulate a strategy for all that needs to be done. After you have visited the remains of the shop let me know what you managed to collect sometime tomorrow. I'll speak to you then. Bye."

He dropped the phone back into its cradle with a sense of relief. Mark was highly competent, a genius electronics man and extremely well organised. With Mark handling the salvage operation, and anything else that could crop up, he himself was for the moment relieved of the immediate aftermath.

As he drank the last of his coffee, the only thing he could think of was bed; and feeling completely washed out, it was a most attractive proposition.

He made the bedroom on legs that would have suited a ninety year old. He didn't even bother to undress; instead he lay down next to Carol, pulled the excess duvet over him and almost immediately fell into a deep sleep.

He awoke with a start, suddenly mindful and pre-occupied with the scenes he had witnessed in the early hours of the morning. A wave of despair flooded his whole body as the enormity of what he was facing in the coming months weighed in on him.

Looking to the bedside clock it read 11.00 a.m. and he realised that Mark should have been in contact by now to report what he had been able to do. In the absence of any contact he knew he would have to drive back to the shop and establish what was going on. It was something he didn't relish – the more he saw the more depressing it would become. And yet, he was obliged to do it – there was no choice.

He turned his head to his left, seeing Carol's figure and surprised she had not moved or stirred since he had laid down six hours before. Pulling himself up and leaning on one elbow he looked down at her and with a shock that hit him like a sledgehammer saw the bloodless colour of her face.

Looking over her at the bedside table he froze, incredulous at the sight of three empty blister packs of Paracetemol and Aspirin. With an anguished cry of 'Oh, dear God' he jumped off the bed and ran around to her side. He rolled her onto her back, aghast at the ashen white skin and the reddened, half closed eyes. In utter disbelief he cradled her head in his arms looking down at her face. Despite the pallid drained colour, it was the most tranquil and worry free she had looked in a long time. The only sign of distress on her now lifeless form was the white, powdery dribble of crushed tablets and saliva coming from one corner of her mouth.

He felt the chill of her cold body in his arms and as hope drained from him he let his emotions flood out. His head fell back, and with tears starting to leak from his eyes he screamed at the heavens "I hate you, how I bloody hate you!"

With that he folded forward onto her body, and wept.

2

The ensuing days and weeks were black.

Somehow he stumbled though each terrible, sombre and interminable day hardly aware of what was happening or what he was doing. He would awake each morning not knowing if he had any reason to live, and wondering why he even bothered to stagger through each grim, nightmarish night.

If he slept, it was through shear exhaustion, if he dressed it was thought force of habit, if he ate it was because it distracted him from the constant emptiness in his soul.

He began to see everything through a packet of Corn Flakes; for breakfast, lunch and evening meals – it was all he could stomach. He was in a deep and permanent shock. He found it impossible to surface; almost every waking minute was filled with a sorrow it was impossible to shrug off. Indeed, Carol's memory left so huge a hole in his soul that after her loss nothing else seemed to matter. At the funeral he was utterly distraught, his emotions crushed to near insanity. His life became dream like, he hardly registered what was happening and if he did, he didn't care.

Mark Stapleford would occasionally arrive at the house to guide him through encounters with doctors, agents and officials, most of whom he instantly forgot the moment a meeting or an engagement was over. He was prescribed pills that he munched habitually with his Corn Flakes, not knowing why he took them or what they were for.

Months passed, and only slowly did he begin to notice the world around him.

The dark oblivion that he had submerged into began to forsake him, and reluctantly he started to become responsive to what was taking place around him. Slowly, very slowly, he surfaced.

As time refurbishing the shop allowed, Mark would take him out, insisting that a walk and the chance of a conversation would do him good. Occasionally he would return home having no recollection of where they had been or what they had done. It never seemed to deter Mark who took the view that even if he could contrive only a moments distraction from his friends grim memories, it was wholly therapeutic and well worth the time.

It was only when Mark and he were walking past his old shop that he suddenly realised where they were. For once his attention was completely taken and he became distracted from his brooding and melancholy state.

Mark stopped in front of the first window but said nothing; he simply waited to see what the reaction would be.

"Mark – is this?"

"Yeah Eddy, it's your shop."

"But it's gone – it was... nothing left!"

"Your right, months ago it was well and truly wrecked, and it took some doing to restore everything. When you were *non compis*...I mean, you have a lot of friends Eddy and while you were recovering we managed to arrange all that needed to be done to get things off the ground. It took five months but we re-opened two weeks ago. Why don't you pop in and have a look around, I'm sure you'll find it just the way you like it."

"But Mark, all the paperwork, the insurances, the re-stocking – God that's a brand new *Thermio-Tec* power amplifier in the window – they have a nine month lead time on them. How on earth did you..."

Mark grinned, "As I said, you have a lot of friends Eddy – when everyone heard what had happened they all bent over backwards to get the stock replaced – nearly all the famous manufacturers diverted orders from one particular customer to us – we got preferential treatment all the way down the line. I hope you'll notice that this window display is exactly as it was before those bastard ram raiders hit us – in fact just after the raid I did as you asked, and managed to salvage a good deal of stuff. After I cleaned it all up and carried out operational and safety checks a significant number went back on the shelves. The insurers weren't aware of the recovery so we got compensated for the full stock list – I'm sure you will be more than delighted to know that."

For the first time in a very long time he smiled, aware that Mark had said the one thing that could cheer him up.

"Thanks Mark – I can't tell you how grateful I am for your loyalty and hard work. I promise you, not only my sincere gratitude but I will, as soon as possible, reward you for what you have done."

Mark grinned, "There was a little selfishness in it Eddy – a lot of us were dependent on getting things running again – our livelihoods were at stake. That said, I'm afraid we lost Tom Perry and Neville Clark from sales, they were unable to subsist on half pay. Janice and Maureen both stayed on and are still in the office. I replaced Tom and Neville with two good replacements both of whom were with *Audio Max* at one time. Oh yes, something else, I put a couple of very competent people in the workshop while I was managing things and waiting for you to take over again. I'm not sure you will want to keep them on indefinitely but at the moment our turnover says we can afford it. Our sales and service since we re-opened are triple what they were."

He stood looking into the shop window, and for the first time in months he was not consumed or pre-occupied by all the terrible past events. Rather he was astonished by the pristine look of the two shop facades, the gleaming and well-displayed products in the windows and the expectation and excitement of being alive again.

He smiled at Mark Stapleford, "Lead on Mark, I'm at your service."

Mark grinned, "You forget chief, we all owe you a lot. As your employees will tell you, your kindness and consideration, in the face of a lot of shit will never be forgotten. Come on then."

As the glass doors opened, and he walked in behind Mark he found himself surrounded by a scene he never thought he would see again. It was almost as if he had time-shifted back to before the ram raid, as if his recollections of that time had been plucked from his memory and given substance and reality.

It was uncanny – as he stopped inside the right hand entrance of the shop and surveyed the shelves, the display cabinets and the general décor, it was as thought nothing had ever been smashed, crushed or reduced to fragments. Even the distribution of all the audio products and sundry accessories was virtually as he remembered it, so too the shop décor, beautifully restored and in the same colour tones as before. It smelt new, it all looked new and it started to restore his optimism.

Mark turned and beckoned him on.

There were four customers in the shop and clearly more elsewhere because he could dimly hear the second movement of Beethoven's 5th leaking out from the listening room. As he hesitated, taking in the quality of sound reaching his ears, the two new staff members came forward and stood somewhat sheepishly in front of the central display cabinet.

"Mr. Lincoln, may I introduce Sam Hill and Peter Lansdale – both new here but even in their short time with us each has demonstrated a professional attitude, excellent customer relationship and in every respect promising to be an asset to the firm."

The two young men both flushed slightly with embarrassment but said nothing.

He shook hands with both of them "You'll forgive me if we don't get to know one another immediately, I'm going to be part time for a while but I promise we'll have a chat as soon as possible. We've always had a good team here – I hope you'll be happy at Lincoln's"

The two men nodded in appreciation and then turned away as Mark indicated a move.

"Thought you'd like to see your office and the other sections – just to put your mind at rest that is. After you." He gave a slight bow in the direction of the door leading away from the central display counter. There were three doors leading away from the interior of the shop, one led to his old office. He made for the office door with a slight trepidation – the last time he'd been in the shop everything was nothing but destruction. But as he pushed against the self-closing door, what he saw before him left him astonished once more. His office was as he remembered it, entirely untouched. There was no dust; no debris and even the papers he had been processing on that last Friday afternoon were still on his desk.

He heard the door close softly behind him as Mark entered.

"Thing is Eddy, the raiders ignored your office, the workshop, admin office and the stock room. Why I can't say – maybe it was

CHAPTER 2

time – too much to go through and too little time to do it before they felt they might be caught. So, as best we can judge, no one came in here – when I checked on that Saturday morning after the raid your office here was intact, so too the stock room and the admin' office. They had a go at the workshop but took nothing, finding most of the stuff in pieces."

It was an amazing revelation; in his mind he had envisaged total devastation with hardly anything left untouched or not smashed.

He ran his eyes over everything, the certificates, the photographs and the familiarity of the room, which at one time had bespoke security, progress and a lifestyle that included a loving wife and home.

Carol's picture on his desk caused him to suddenly flood with emotion but somehow he held it in check. He sat at his desk cupping his chin in his hands and switching his mind to something else to relieve himself of the instantaneous sadness.

"Mark, I don't understand how you organised all this without me. Surely you had to deal with a lot of legal problems staff payments and so on – not to mention the insurance and stock re-ordering. How did you manage it?"

Mark smiled "I think you tend to forget that when you started the business here seven years ago you gave your lawyers power of attorney, you never rescinded it. I'm sure you hardly registered any of it, but all those meetings I dragged you to recently when you were...er' recovering...were to ensure you were there to back up what I was doing to salvage things. We – that is the lawyers and myself – negotiated the insurance settlement, the contracts for the re-stock, payments for the shop refurbishment and a control charge on your bank accounts and the business account. In the end it all came to fruition – painfully, but it happened."

For a moment he was speechless with astonishment.

"God...well done Mark, but where do we stand now. I see the marvellous miracle you've worked but what about our public liability insurance, the insurance cover for the shop, overnight security, our obligations to suppliers and so on. Are we safe now?"

Mark sat down opposite him and leaned back in the chair.

We've fitted bar shutters to the front of the shop – they are supposedly ram proof – they're certainly far tougher than the mesh shutters we had before; but let's face it, if they use a tank or a bulldozer they'll get thought. Our previous CCTV system was useless – that's been rectified. As for insurance, well...we do have some but it won't cover everything like the previous cover – the new insurance has too many exceptions for comfort. However, financially we have come out of it fairly well. As I implied earlier, since we re-opened we are operating very profitably, there was a lot of pent up trade it seems. Add to that the insurance compensation, and our very kind and generous suppliers, and it turns out the business is remarkably solvent. You're reserves were able to keep us going while everything got sorted out. As I said, for that, and your kindness to us, we will be forever grateful."

As he heard Mark speak, he gave thanks to God that he had hired such an enormously able, responsible and competent man. Mark and he had always got on well, but he was almost brought to tears to realise that Mark had saved the business. He could only guess at the hassle Mark had overcome to reach the stage they were at.

"Mark, saying thank you isn't enough – I can't tell you how much I appreciate all that you have done, I..."

There was a soft knock at his door, repeated again gently in the same staccato way.

Mark turned.

"I think I know who that might be."

"Come in."

The door opened, not fully, but enough for two women to slip in. One, tall and conservatively dressed in a flower decked dress, the other smaller, younger, dressed in a flame skirt and matching top. They stood smiling as the door shut silently behind them.

He was delighted – his two office administrators Janice and Maureen had appeared holding a vase of flowers and a potted plant.

"Hello Mr. Lincoln," Janice said, "we are so pleased to see you back. We are so sorry about, um...your bereavement...Carol...everything... we thought you would like something to brighten your office so we..."

Maureen stood horrified that Janice had mentioned Carol and gave her a slight push with her elbow.

"Where would you like them?" Maureen interjected.

He stood up, delighted to see the endearing and familiar faces of his long-term employees and in no way hurt by Janice's Freudian slip. He pointed to a long low book cabinet positioned along one side of the office.

"Hello you two, you're a sight for sore eyes – so pleased to see you. Look, pop the flowers and the plant down over there on the table – I'm discussing things with Mark at the moment but I promise I will come and see you both before I leave."

They quickly did as suggested and with shy smiles, and a wave from Janice, returned to the door and left.

He turned back to Mark.

"As I was saying, you've done a stupendous job. I can't begin to tell you how sorry I am that I was so engrossed in my own self-pity that I simply couldn't begin to see any return to normality. I was convinced that what had happened here was irremediable. I

15

assumed that all that was left was the situation before Carol…that is, before it happened."

Mark shifted in his seat – slightly embarrassed by what he was hearing.

"It's okay chief, I…"

"No, it's not okay. You saved my business and you saved my sanity. I want you to take a partnership with me. We'll go 50/50 on the business. What I get you get, straight down the middle? We will see the lawyers over the next week and get it formalised. I hope my offer will convince you of my gratitude. By the way, are you still fiddling in the workshop?"

Mark sat completely stunned by the offer and found it hard to respond.

"Okay Eddy, but we all pulled together you know; not only because we valued you and the business, but it was our livelihoods we were saving. As for the workshop, we've been inundated with equipment for test and repair. You'll have to meet my two guys – I'm pleased to say they know their stuff and are working wonders. Personally, I'm handling two original 1949 *Leak* point ones and, would you believe it, a 1934 *Williamson* amplifier, all of them very interesting challenges. We have three post-war *Wurlitzer* jukebox amplifiers on the go and umpteen solid-state integrated amplifiers and auxiliary devices from the last twenty years. You know me, I revel in this kind of stuff so please don't ask me to take on a purely sales or admin job. I'm not going to be happy outside of my expertise."

He smiled inwardly; as if he would, or could, make Mark do something he was reluctant to do.

"Understood Mark, truth is you undervalue yourself, you're skilled enough and experienced enough to take on any task is this business. However, you do what you want to do. I say that because I know from past events that you are as good a salesman as you are a trouble-shooter. As my partner I have no authority to insist you do anything other than what you want to do. Is that okay?"

Mark nodded and grinned in appreciation.

He was about to get up and keep his appointment with Janice and Maureen when a thought occurred to him.

"Mark – the police – did we get any feedback on the bastards that hit us last time?"

Mark stood up and shook his head.

"Not a sausage, we got the full forensic examination and I was in touch with CID for a while, but nothing came of it. They found the land cruiser they used to ram their way in. It was burnt out – stolen of course. CID thought the raiders were a European gang; that is, from what little could be gleaned from the CCTV video. But the video quality was so bad it amounted to being useless. All I hope is that we don't see them again."

He nodded his agreement with what Mark had said but felt a cold hand clutch his spine.

3

It was a familiar routine and he slipped back into it without much in the way of regret – at least he was alive again. For a while he only popped into the shop for a couple of days in every week for essential administration. As time passed and the open wounds of grief and self-pity became a sad and faded memory, with even the placing of flowers on Carol's headstone becoming an emotional but tearless routine, he was able to resume his old commitments and took over from Mark as the senior manager. Mark, happy to have the same seniority but grateful that he was now able to retire to the workshop, was hardly to be seen or in attendance.

The constant influx of visiting customers, requests for specialist repairs, email queries for bespoke equipment and sales through the internet began to enthral everyone with a sense of success and he was pleased to see the energy and optimism that pervaded everyone and everything the staff were involved with.

In truth there was very little he himself needed to do to inspire, motivate or promote what was being done successfully already. Mark whistled happily on the odd occasion he vacated his workshops, the two new boys, Sam and Peter, quickly took on a professional approach to customer interaction (they cynically called it 'grooming') and from all this profitability increased, enabling an already successful and solvent business to become even more solvent.

Although he had a nagging feeling that he was tempting fate, and it was all too good to last (he remembered King Solomon's dictate 'All things must pass') nevertheless, the business was now definitely on a high and there was no reason to stop him asking 'what next'. It was strange territory, never before had he the time, or the luxury, to think of how he might expand the business and move on to yet greener pastures. Nonetheless, if it was to happen, now was the time. He'd have to consult Mark of course but it was unlikely he would object, particularly if he were promised an expansion of his operations – yes, especially that!

He walked into the workshop to find Mark deep in conversation with one of his engineers. He realised he'd never kept his promise and offered the courtesy of meeting either of the two new people Mark had hired. It was time to kill two birds with one stone.

Each of the men, Robert and David, seemed very young to him but he quickly came to accept their enthusiasm for their discipline. They were well trained in electronics and very knowledgeable about their subject – even to the point of having a well-informed and authoritative perspective on earlier technologies. That, he understood was why Mark had hired them. They appeared pleasant, dependable and self-assured and he took to them both, even though in dress and appearance they were deeply unconventional.

Or was his perspective wrong?

Robert favoured jeans, an open neck shirt and what seemed to be one of his father's tank tops. David had the look of a reformed Hell's Angel, sporting black leather everywhere, even down to his trousers. His belt, with the skull's head buckle, holding his lower gear together, was less than endearing. Yet in conversation, each had the stamp of someone you could depend on. He added competence in electronics to a likeable, if not charming, character in each case. Mark it seemed had chosen well.

As the pleasantries ended he took Mark aside and asked him to come to his office as soon as he had finished; only five minutes elapsed before he heard a knock on his door.

Mark smiled as he closed the office door. "Hope this isn't a 'I know I said you could do as you pleased but would you be prepared to' discussion."

He gestured to the seat in chair in front of him, Mark was in for a pleasing revelation – he hoped.

"Not quite Mark but I wanted your thoughts on an idea of mine." Mark sat down slowly as he offered the counter to Marks query. "I'm listening."

"Okay, for one reason or another we're doing well but we have to ask ourselves where we are going with the business and if we are content to let things stay as they are. The *status quo* is the safe approach we might agree; expansion is what we could go for but it has its risks. Now, I'm not simply talking about opening another shop somewhere, or aiming for a national chain of shops, what I am inclined to is beginning our own brand of equipment – that is, we start to manufacture high grade stuff and develop a personal reputation for top end audio."

Mark looked dumbstruck.

"Golly, do you know what you are saying Eddy? Opening another series of shops we can do, I'm sure, but setting up our own brand…that's something else."

"Where's the harm in asking the question Mark – that's why I'm talking to you. What I want to know is what would it take – is it a practicable proposition? Remember, it doesn't necessarily mean setting up and tooling up a factory from scratch, all we have to do is provide the bespoke circuitry and get some other outfit to manufacture for us. That would be the lowest aspect – it could develop from that."

Mark looked pensive but there was no shaking of his head and no droop of his shoulders to indicate the idea was out of the question.

"Well, if you put it like that Eddy, I always wanted to develop and manufacture some amplifier circuits I designed. I'm sure with a little tweaking they could become commercial."

"Good, and expansion of the shops?"

"No objection – there are areas around London where we could do very well."

He was relieved at Mark's approval of the proposals. Now all he had to do was start the process.

"Okay Mark – have a think of where we might begin the 'own brand' series, and if you have noticed any sites where you thought we could be successful give me a list. I'm going to be around for the rest of the week and then I'm going to see what you and others might recommend as a good place for a new business. Agreed?"

Mark nodded, his face betraying some excitement.

"Would be great to have our own stuff – Lincoln Audio, sounds good. See you later then."

As Mark rose and exited the office he had a thought.

"No Mark, were partners and if it's using your designs it will be *Lincoln-Stapleford Audio*."

Mark's smile beamed his agreement.

He'd been disappointed over the last few days. He travelled in an almost circular route around the M25 running from the south of the London boroughs all the way up through Essex and down past Epping, Dartford, Otford and back to Redhill; each point acting as a base for inward incursions towards central

London. Local agents had supplied wads of specifications of available commercial premises, and as he laboriously worked his way through them he left behind a trial of discarded paper, each signifying a failed viewing. It was only when by accident he inadvertently lost his sense of direction and ignoring the 'satnav' ended up in Guildford that he saw an opportunity. All that he had seen so far had been vacant shops that were vacant for the wrong reason - very poor location, too much competition or entirely away from the main stream of shoppers and viewers. But the one he saw for leasehold in Guildford was perfectly positioned with, even on a Tuesday afternoon, throngs of people passing by on a busy high street. As a University town it promised a permanently swollen population constantly changing and bringing in fresh interest. He wasted no time in approaching the agents and was promised an almost immediate viewing.

Mark Stapleford viewed the relatively customer denuded state of the shop with a degree of thankfulness. He disliked having to do any faultfinding while too many customers were in the shop. It offended his sense of order and neatness, and usually interfered with his concentration. The current problem was an intermittent connection on the speaker-switching panel that allowed any one amplifier to be paired with any set of loudspeakers. Because it was not in the listening room, which only exhibited the most select and sophisticated systems, he was working in the main display area. It was in his haste, and his reluctance not to clutter the pristine appearance of the shop, that he began to make mistakes. First he dropped his multi-meter, smashing the battery compartment and forcing him to get another meter from the workshop. Then he spent ten minutes tracing a lost signal only to find that the source amplifier was actually switched off.

Thereafter he found himself struggling with a signal that came and went but not for any obvious reason. He was about to conclude that the amplifier itself was actually faulty when he heard shouts from Sam Hill and Peter Lansdale.

Mark looked across the open floor between the display shelves and the counters and saw the two men by the entrance struggling with a youth. He was dressed in the usual street uniform – trainers, jeans and a 'hoody'. The youth was clutching a box and fighting back with his free right hand, swinging it like a club at the two sales assistants. They in turn were attempting to evade the swings and grapple with him. As one of the men stepped back to avoid another swing, the youth dropped the box.

His hair was dark brown and long and flicked around as he fought to get to the double glass doors open to exit the shop. As the two assistants moved in again he turned and pulled out a long, wicked looking kitchen knife from his pocket.

The two froze, not wanting to tempt a more aggressive move from someone threatening them with a lethal looking blade. The youth held it forward, first one way and then the other, threatening Sam and Peter in turn.

As this took place Mark decided to intervene and ran forward still carrying the test meter in one hand and the two-wire connected probes in the other. He approached the youth whose wild-eyed look promised little in the way of compromise.

"Fuck off or I'll do you."

Mark straightened and stepped forward one more pace.

"No you won't – you'll have to get all three of us and that you won't do."

He looked down at the box lying on the floor.

"Is it worth it for a pair of earphones? Do you want to turn petty theft into murder? Drop the knife and you are unlikely to face really serious charges. Come on, be sensible."

Out of the corner of his eye he saw that Sam and Peter had stood their ground so he was confident of his earlier statement.

Suddenly the youth expertly threw the knife from one hand to the other, instantly sweeping it in a long backward arc. He had a long reach and the end of the blade caught Sam Hill's cheek and cut deeply across to his chin. Sam jerked back, caught by the pain from the injury and horrified by the blood spurting onto his fingers.

The youth sneered. "You two next."

As the youth brought the knife back round towards Mark and Peter, Sam Hill suddenly reacted. With a cry of anger and outrage he dived forward and snatched at the hand holding the knife. As he moved the youth tried to twist the blade in his direction.

Mark immediately realised that Sam was in mortal danger – his timing as he attempted to grab the hand was too slow; the knife had flicked up and was moving towards his stomach.

There was no choice – gripping the test probe like a dagger he stabbed it point forward into the side of the youth. As it punched though clothing and deep into flesh the youth gasped and instantly convulsed. Then, folding forward into a virtual foetal position he collapsed towards the floor. The wire, linking the test meter and the probe, was short. As the youth fell, Mark, still holding tightly to the meter, saw the wire go taut and tear itself away from where he had driven the probe in. He stepped back to avoid the falling body and as the wire pulled away the broken end of the probe dragged across the carpet leaving a few spots of blood.

For a moment no one moved and apart from a distant background of music playing in the listening room there was near silence. The youth had made no noise as he collapsed and from the ashen colour of his face he was in shock.

Peter Lansdale suddenly said "Hell! That was close Mark."

He found it hard to register what had happened – it was instinctive, and the only thing he could do to protect Sam.

Sam, with copious amounts of blood dribbling between the fingers pressed against his face, looked aghast and managed an "Oh God." as he bent down to look at the fallen youth.

Mark tried to get some composure back.

"Peter, call 999 – we need an ambulance and the police. Quick please."

For a moment Peter Lansdale hesitated, still aghast and mesmerised by the event – then he turned away and ran for the telephone.

There was little they could do, the probe was buried deep inside the youth and they made no attempt to disturb it. He was unconscious from the moment he hit the floor and remained so for the time it took for the emergency services to arrive. As the three watched the ambulance accelerate away with sirens blaring, Mark held on to the earphone box that was central to the shoplifting episode. Soon the police would arrive and be asking questions, and he was in no way looking forward to it.

Wasn't it a shit end to the day?

4

It was becoming a long session with the estate agents. The leasing, ground rent, local taxes and utility costs were piling up and he was attempting to make a decision without any prior knowledge of what the refurbishment, stocking and staffing costs might be. He certainly needed to establish the 'pros and cons' quickly; there was no doubt he was in competition with other interested parties and if he was going to take on the lease of the Guildford shop he had to decide as soon as possible.

On paper, and given the shop's location, it had a lot going for it and if he took it on it was hardly going to be the mistake of the century. And yet he was still unsure of why the previous occupants had vacated the premises; the agents were somewhat vague about what had happened, citing a family breakdown of some sort. Not only that the turnover figures were unimpressive; though because the shop had traded in wool and baby clothes it could explain the poor showing.

Now he sat at the agents desk, sipping a third cup of coffee and wondering if he should simply get up, go home, and chew over his decision at leisure. Of course, he would be taking the risk of finding himself regretting not seizing the opportunity while he could, especially if someone beat him to it – but as his mother had once said, 'decide in haste, repent at leisure'. He also recalled the contrary 'faint heart never won fair maiden'.

As he grew weary of the indecision plaguing him, he felt his mobile vibrate to indicate an incoming message. Just as he was about to view what had arrived it also began to chime for attention.

He pressed the accept button, muted the amplifier for privacy and with the phone at his ear listened. "Hello, Mr. Lincoln, hello? It's Maureen – Oh, Mr. Lincoln something terrible has happened! A man has been stabbed in the shop – yes, Mark stabbed a man! The police were here and Mark, Sam and Peter are under arrest. Oh! I don't know what to do – Mark said to phone you. Can you get back?"

He stood by the agents desk utterly bewildered, stunned and shaken by the news and hardly able to register its credibility.

"Dear Christ Maureen, how the hell did that happen? Do you mean Mark...stabbed...they are all under arrest? I simply can't believe what you are saying. How did it...? Look, stay in the shop, close up and I will be with you soon – I'm in Guildford, it should take me no more than an hour if I can beat the rush hour. Is that okay, can you stay on for a while?"

He heard a sob at the end of the line and then she said, "Yes – I'll be here, what about Janice, can she go home?"

"Yes, unless she can add to what you know."

"I don't think so – no, I don't think so."

Again, he heard a sob and a nose being blown.

"All right Maureen, I'm on my way."

As he closed his phone the estate agent reappeared. "Everything all right Mr. Lincoln? I'm sorry, I couldn't help overhearing."

He shook his head. "No, major problems I'm afraid. Look, I'm going to have to shelve my interest in the shop. If my circumstances change I'll contact you. I'm sorry for your trouble."

He turned on his heel and rapidly exited the estate agents

offices. As he made for the car park and his car, he had one thing on his mind. He knew Mark Stapleford and the boys very well. There had to be an innocent explanation for all this and he was not only going to expose it but as far as his staff were concerned he was not about to let any one of them down.

It took less than fifty minutes to get back to the shop but it seemed like fifty hours. Every traffic jam, every red light and every dawdling driver increased the frustration. His mind went through every possible scenario that could have turned Mark Stapleford into a weapon-wielding maniac. The more he pondered on it, the more ridiculous the whole thing appeared. No way would Mark stab someone unless in extremis. It was impossible unless it was self-defence, and even then he doubted its veracity. Soon he would know, he was only two minutes from the shop.

He pulled in to his parking bay behind the shop and exited the car as fast as possible. He banged hard on the metal security door knowing Maureen would have locked it. After a seemingly endless time he heard the lock being defeated and the door opened.

Maureen stood aside as he brushed past her and he watched in silence as she closed the door behind him. As she turned towards him her tear-streaked face told him of her distress. Red eyed and still crying, she simply stood in front of him, shaking her head and with her arms open in an appeal for comfort. He took her in his arms and hugged her, letting her cry into his shoulder. Then he locked eyes with her and smiled. "It's okay. Come into the office – we'll make some tea and then you can tell me what happened." She nodded thankfully and followed him through the stock room and into the showroom where the office door was located. He stood watching the tearful woman drop into the chair opposite his desk.

"Stay here Maureen, I'll get some tea, I won't..."

She turned, "There's a pot full in the admin office - on the side by the third filing cabinet. Milk's in the fridge."

He smiled in gratitude - he was in no condition to struggle with searching for tea bags, milk or sugar.

"Okay, hang on I'll be back soon."

5

The tea was a tonic to his drained and adrenalin soaked body, even Maureen appeared slightly refreshed; nevertheless, it was only a temporary respite.

"Tell me what you know – or were told."

She took breath and gave a timid smile.

"I only saw the aftermath – a young man lying on the floor unconscious –well, he was deathly pale and not moving at all. Mark was standing in front of him holding a test meter with a wire trailing down to the ground. Peter and Sam were standing on Marks left and right standing around the man on the floor. Oh, yes – there was a box, *Bose* earphones; it was close to the man on the ground. Mark retrieved it."

"Right Maureen, so you didn't see any of the incident itself?"

She looked shamed. " No Mr. Lincoln, I didn't. But I spoke to Peter Lansdale afterwards, he told me what had happened."

"Okay Maureen, tell me what he said."

She looked up, as if collecting her thoughts.

"It seems that the first Peter knew about it was when he heard Sam tell the youth not to leave the shop. On the face of it the man was shoplifting otherwise Sam would not have challenged him. Peter turned to see Sam barring the way of a 'hoody' as he put it, who was holding the earphones. Peter went forward to help and the man turned on them brandishing a long knife. Sam and Peter backed away and Peter said they tried to reason with him but he took no notice; instead he kept menacing them with the knife. Then Mark appeared and confronted the youth. In his haste to arrive at the argument, Mark was still carrying a test meter. The man became even more agitated as Mark tried to calm him down and eventually he swung the blade against Sam's face. Sam was slit along the cheek and chin and started bleeding badly. As this happened Mark drove a test probe against the youth's body to stop him doing anymore damage. It penetrated deeply and the youth fainted. Mark told Peter to call an ambulance and the police. While we all waited, Janice and I put dressings on Sam's chin – he was bleeding a lot. The ambulance arrived a good while before the police and after the paramedics attended them the shoplifter and Sam were taken off to hospital. After the police arrived they asked to see the CCTV pictures and Mark took them into the stock room where the camera recorders were. Not long after viewing the video Mark and Peter were arrested; they were handcuffed here in the shop ...and later Sam was arrested when he was discharged from casualty at the hospital. That's all I know at the moment."

He sighed and whispered a profanity to himself.

Sorry Mr. Lincoln – what did you say?"

He looked at Maureen with some sympathy.

"Nothing my love, I was simply thinking that sometimes it never rains but it pours. Thank you for staying on and thanks for your report. You can go home now. When you come in tomorrow have the lads in the workshop stand in for Sam and Peter. No repairs – the workshop can stay closed for now. All of us, I suspect, will need some help tomorrow. You and Janice keep your normal routine. Okay?"

Maureen smiled. "Okay, no problem. What are you going to do?"

He hesitated but knew he was obliged to do something and that something had to be done as soon as possible.

"I'm going to have a word with the police and it's going to be very loud and very offensive."

He managed to park close to the police station; in fact he could see it across the road from where he had left the car. It was an old Victorian building with its façade made of smoke stained, dark brown brickwork, giving it a dark and forbidding appearance. Even the outside lighting was fitted with low wattage lamps that could do no more than flood the steps leading up to the ancient glazed mahogany doors with a gloomy and brooding light. Even the two streetlights on each side of the pavement seemed sad and dejected.

As he entered through the swing doors his nose detected a fetid, fusty atmosphere, rank with the reactions of all those innumerable people who were now, or had been, incarcerated in the cells. As he passed the notice boards adorned with warnings about home security, wanted felons and appeals for witnesses to accidents, he almost missed the archway opening on to the enquiry desk. As a dark blue uniform caught his attention he turned and saw that the desk sergeant on duty was Neilson who gave a nod of recognition as he approached the desk.

"Good evening Mr. Lincoln, I wondered how long it would be before we saw you. I imagine you have a lot of questions."

"Yes I have, the first is what the hell are you doing keeping my people in custody. As I understand it they were simply defending themselves against a knife-wielding shoplifter. I want them out, now!"

Neilson gave a sympathetic look.

"I don't think your employees will be released on bail just yet, the station Superintendent has issued a 36 hour detainment order while further investigations are made. Which is why you weren't contacted immediately. Right now there are three lawyers talking to the three in custody, if you..."

He was too tired for any fobbing off, the whole bloody thing was ridiculous.

"For God's sake sergeant – what on earth requires further investigation, it's a clear case of ..."

Neilson shook his head to interrupt the tirade.

"Mr. Lincoln, I think it might be better if you talk to Detective Sergeant Moran, he has a better perspective on things than I have. Hold on, I'll get him for you."

It occurred to him to say no more – the higher up the ladder he got the more likely he was to get clarification and something done. Neilson picked up a phone and pressed a button on the call pad.

He turned away, listening to Neilson explain matters to an unknown recipient and studying the scuffed and worn out floor tiles around the enquiry desk. He wondered how many thousands of other anxious visitors had stood in the same spot and paced away yet more of the floor surface.

"Sergeant Moran's on his way Mr. Lincoln – he'll be right down."

He turned to acknowledge Neilson's confirmation and went towards the desk.

"Come on sergeant, you know me, surely you can...."

"Mr. Lincoln – I'm D.S. Moran, would you care to follow me?"

He was startled by the unexpected loudness of the voice. He looked to his right into an adjoining corridor, seeing a man in

33

his fifties with greying hair standing some ten yards from him. Moran was heavily built and dressed in a dark suit, white shirt and a florid tie.

He responded with a surprised "Yes, I'm coming."

Moran waited until he they were abreast and then began to walk alongside.

"There's an interview room we can use just along here – not too far."

Moran gave a genuine smile – he hoped it was favourable.

They entered a large, virtually square, high-ceilinged room containing only a long wooden table and four chairs nestling neatly under it. On the wall, close to the table was a shelf on which sat a voice recorder, a digital clock and an untidy stack of papers. The room had a distinct odour, old cigarettes, human sweat and an atmosphere of hopelessness. Even the walls had given up; their once brilliant white emulsion had over the years succumbed to incessant streams of cigarette smoke and had now turned to a dismal dark amber.

He sat down at one of the chairs and waited for Moran to do the same opposite him.

"I imagine you need updating on the situation with your employees Mr. Lincoln."

He leaned forward. "That sergeant is an understatement – if what I heard is correct you have no right to be holding my people."

Moran clasped his hands together as if to placate him.

"Look, the three we have in custody are there for a very good reason – given the seriousness of the charges we can't offer police bail – they have to appear before the magistrates tomorrow to face a decision for a Crown Court commitment. "

He couldn't believe his ears.

"What did you say, serious charges? What the hell for? As I was told, it was a case of self-defence. Who the hell do you think you are dealing with here? My people are decent, hard working..."

Moran held up the palm of his hand stopping him in mid flow.

"Mr. Lincoln, I suspect you are not fully aware of the facts. Let me enlighten you. First, it's not our decision; in these cases the Crown Prosecution Service decide what process we follow. The CPS decide what must be done on the available evidence and I have to say, given the video we have seen showing what took place, there can be no doubt that the charges are appropriate."

Hearing Moran's casual remark about 'charges', he could hardly contain himself.

"Charges Sergeant? What bloody charges, I keep hearing this term as though we are talking about premeditated murder, not self-defence. Just what are they supposed to be guilty of? A bloody shoplifter casually lifts an expensive pair of earphones, gets intercepted, pulls out a knife, seriously wounds one of my employees lawfully involved with an arrest, threatens two others and gets a bit of his own medicine in return. Tell me where the incident warrants my people being locked up and subject to charges?"

Moran looked at his hands as if embarrassed and then replied.

"Mr. Lincoln, I suspect you aren't fully aware of all the facts. First, the man did not shoplift anything; in fact he was returning the earphones for replacement. He'd purchased them from your shop seven months ago, before the unfortunate raid on your premises. We know that's true – the receipt for the earphones was found in his pocket. It seems your shop assistant, Mr. Hill failed to see, or hear, him enter the shop. The video shows that Hill had his back to the door when the customer entered. The customer, having come in to the shop, and then apparently catching sight of a familiar face outside the shop, turned to open the door a fraction to acknowledge the individual. However, at that point Mr. Hill turned and from his perspective the customer was about to leave the shop with unpaid goods...hence the interception."

Moran leaned back in his chair as if to consider what next to say. But it made no difference; as far as he was concerned Moran had justified nothing.

"So what? Innocent or not as far as shoplifting is concerned, the man went berserk and whipped out a knife. He would have created havoc with it had he not been stopped. I note you have not indicated that the video shows him trying to explain the situation. With a receipt he'd nothing to worry about. Instead he goes on a lethal offensive; clearly he was psychotic. I've been told that Sam Hill has a very significant wound on his face and was very near to getting his throat cut. Don't tell me that in those circumstances my people didn't react as any other sane person would. In short, Mark Stapleford responded in self-defence, so lets stop this stupid game – what happened to that man was his own fault. I suggest that you remind the CPS of everything that happened to my people and put the so-called victim behind bars; you can then release my employees."

Moran gave a faint shrug of his wide shoulders.

"Not something we can do, I'm sorry to say Mr. Lincoln. Normally we would have charged the victim with attempted murder – but that's out of the question now. You see, the man died in the ambulance on the way to the hospital. It seems the stab wound he received punctured his only surviving kidney, the only one he had left having had the other kidney removed previously because of a tumour.

Moran's revelation floored him.

"Okay –but what about the recent ruling on excessive force, as I understand it you are entitled to use whatever force is necessary, even if it is excessive, to counter the threat at hand. All my people did was exactly that, counter the threat."

Moran gave a sympathetic smile.

"Yes, but his violent death means that there is an indictable offence and I believe some of your people will have to face manslaughter charges, the others will probably be charged with being an accessory before the fact. You see, in this case the plea of self defence and/or excessive force must be considered in court – not before, and not by the CPS."

Anger flared up inside him and he felt like bursting. Yet, regardless of his fury, he was impotent, his anger was not going to directly change anything. He suppressed his outrage, trying to counter the change in circumstances. Since due process was inevitable it would be better that he ensured the best possible legal defence for his people and ensure that the whole ridiculous travesty be brought out into public view. The newspapers would have a field day pointing to the stupid way the law worked and would particularly scandalise the CPS for its dogged adherence to legal niceties and a brainless and unthinking lack of good sense.

Moran saw the flood of emotion going through him and spoke up.

"If it's any consolation Mr. Lincoln, I doubt any jury in the land will convict your people, and I think the CPS know that. But like all legal dilemmas they feel obliged to prosecute to avoid being seen to ignore or favour certain unlawful acts. There are three solicitors supporting all of your employees. With a decent brief acting for them the various charges will be made to look ridiculous."

He gave Moran a nod of thanks for his final observation.

"Okay sergeant, thank you for that reassurance, but it still strikes me as a huge waste of public and private funds. There has to be a better way – like in France. An investigating magistrate decides if there is sufficient reason to prosecute, if not the case is void. That's what we need. Likewise, a delayed coroner's inquest won't help to clarify matters."

Moran smiled an agreement and started to get up from his chair holding out his hand for a handshake. He proffered his own hand but decided on one last question.

"Just one thing sergeant, you know my business was raided four times – did you ever get a sniff of who was involved."

Moran continued to shake his hand, at the same time looking pensive and for a long few moments said nothing. Then he said, "We got close on the last ram-raid but the bastards were long gone – eastern European we think, and we couldn't track them down. That said, we know the individuals we are dealing with and we're on the lookout for them. All ferry, rail and air terminals have either their real or their photo-fit pictures. Sooner or later...well, you know what I mean!"

He retrieved his hand from Moran's powerful grip and followed him out of the room into the corridor.

Moran gave a "Nice to meet you Mr. Lincoln, I'll keep you posted." and walked away. As he watched Moran walk off he turned and retraced his steps back to the enquiry desk. He suddenly realised that he could no longer smell the station's distinctive odour. He presumed that for most people it was like living on a pig farm, in a short while you habituated to the smell and it vanished. All he hoped was that he could make the present crisis disappear – just like the smell. He wasn't asking for much, just a touch of what he called real justice.

6

It was an unseasonably warm morning and the newly built glass and steel courthouse was stifling. The TV and radio had given a breaking news report on the arrests in their late evening bulletins and it meant that the whole country was virtually aware of what had taken place. The newspapers were late in reporting the case and wanted to be first to get the court hearing into print. Curiously, he'd received no contact from the media at all, but perhaps it really wasn't surprising – the spotlight was on the players in the incident and those individuals now accused.

The courthouse was packed, with media, officials, lawyers and the families and friends of his two employees. The larger contingent was in support of his business partner.

He'd arrived early and managed to get to see all the close family members of Mark Stapleford. He spent as much time as he could with the families, fiancée and girlfriend of the other two men. In every case he assured all involved that no expense would be spared to get the best legal defence possible if the three were committed for trial. In every meeting he had at least received smiles of thanks amongst all the tears and anxiety.

Even now, squashed into the courtroom, awash with officials, onlookers and some of the media, all silently and eagerly awaiting the arraignment, he realised that he was actually on the periphery of all the events – he had not even had a chance to speak to his people or their lawyers. That he intended to remedy as soon as possible.

As the clock approached ten he watched as three magistrates, the senior being a stipendiary magistrate – a lawyer – file in to the high bench facing the court, as they did so the clerk called for silence.

The hubbub in the courtroom subsided into a murmur, instigated by the arrival from a side door of three men, handcuffed and heavily escorted. They filed in and turned to stand in front of the bench.

He was able to get only a fleeting look at the faces of his people, but he could not fail to see the look of resentment each man carried. Sam Hill had half his face obscured by a thick dressing over most of his face which though it only just missed his lips could not hide his grim expression. Just before Peter Lansdale turned towards the magistrates he looked towards the crowd and caught sight of him. He instinctively raised a hand to acknowledge Peter and he received a nod in reply.

As Peter turned away a low sound started from the back of the courtroom; a sound that soon began to swell.

'Shame, shame,' began to be chanted by an ever-increasing number of voices, getting louder and louder and starting to be mixed with clapping.

The three prisoners turned to see what was happening and their faces lit up with the sudden realisation that they had massive public support. He turned to look back and saw all the family members and friends of the three now standing before the magistrates grouped together and leading the chant. Very soon the whole gathering had joined in and it soon became a crescendo of sound that persisted for what seemed like many minutes. It was only when court officials and bailiffs started to intermingle with the family group and attempted to calm them into silence that the mantra began to die.

After some minutes the court had settled, and apart from the typical noises emanating from a crowd of annoyed and restless people, order had been restored. The magistrate's bench had up to now remained unmoved and aloof by the demonstration, but as quite descended on the courtroom the chief magistrate leaned forward.

"Should there be a repeat of this disgraceful behaviour I will clear the court – I hope that is understood. We will proceed. Read the charges!"

A justice's clerk stood and turned to the three men.

"Mark Simon Stapleford, you are charged with manslaughter under common law and part 4 of the 2009 Coroner and Justice Act sections 54 and 55 and of the Police and Criminal Evidence Act, in that on the 14th of this month you did grievously wound one Philip Dighton subsequently causing his death. How do you plead, guilty or not guilty?"

He saw Mark flinch with annoyance but then he straightened and with a strong voice said, "I refuse to plead. This is unjust I…"

The chief magistrate gave a slight twitch of his head and started to speak but anything he or Mark had more to say was drowned out by the reaction of the courtroom as derision and whistles broke out from the watching crowd.

Again, the pandemonium subsided and the charges against Sam Hill and Peter Lansdale were read; and whether it had been agreed between their lawyers beforehand, or they simply took their lead from Mark, each refused to plead. As their response to the charges of 'aiding and abetting before the fact' was an emphatic 'I refuse to plead', a number of voices in the crowd retorted with 'Right', or "Good for you'.

The chief magistrate now sat impassively, waiting for the

procedure to be completed.

As Peter Lansdale's answer to the charges finished, the chief magistrate looked down at the senior justice's clerk and said "Enter a plea of not guilty for all three defendants against all three charges."

As this was said a grey suited man came forward and stood in front of the bench.

"Your worships, I speak for the three accused. Given the extraordinary circumstances surrounding this case, and the widespread media interest, I submit that for the interim bail should be set. All three men here are of impeccably good character. The charges are ludicrous and there is no risk of them absconding should this matter be put before the next assizes."

The chief magistrate scowled and leaned to his left and right consulting the two 'wingers', the two lay juniors on the bench. He turned back to face the lawyer. "Given the seriousness of the charges, and the attitude of the accused, we cannot agree. The charges are outside the jurisdiction of this court, accordingly the accused will be remanded in custody to appear before the crown court in Winchester at the first available date."

For a second or two an icy silence filled the courtroom, the onlookers momentarily bewildered and unable to grasp the decision.

Then a near riot broke out as some of the crowd shouted contempt at the magistrates. One loud voice screamed, "You should have dismissed the case you morons, the CPS don't know what the hell they are doing." It was a sentiment apparently shared by the majority in attendance many of whom refused to move as court officials tried to eject them.

Personally, he had no reason to stay any longer in the court, he knew full well that the magistrate's decision against the three men would not be reversed, regardless of the behaviour he had just witnessed.

He painstakingly wound his way out through the throngs of arguing people, noting as he exited the court entrance that the whole area was packed with cameras of all kinds – TV, photographic and phone – all supported by communications personnel. They too vented their frustration on the court officials because all of them had been refused access to anywhere near the inside of the court. For all the uproar and bustle he managed to slip past every reporter, camera crew and relay unit, and made his way to the overflow car park. It too was crammed to capacity with not a single parking bay free. Yet the car park area was surprisingly quiet, hardly a soul in sight; apparently the whole town and innumerable others had migrated to the court. It gave testament to how much interest and divergence of opinion the case had caused.

As he drove back home he felt a deep sympathy for his people. Even if they were eventually acquitted they would still have been unfairly imprisoned for the time between their arrest and their appearance in the Crown court. Not only that, they would have endured the anxiety of not knowing if due process would see justice done.

As that thought arose, he gave a snort of derision; 'justice done' was not what he called it. Tomorrow he would seek the best defence counsel he could – someone not afraid to take on the system and show it up to be stupid, dogmatic and anomalous. He wanted his people acquitted and freed and he wanted the bloody system to apologise. After that, he would campaign for a better and more pragmatic way.

7

Nathan Elliot QC's London office was housed in a large Georgian block filled with the legal chambers of his competitors – for Nathan Elliot subscribed to the rule that it was safer to keep your enemies closer to you than your friends. His bulk virtually filled the high-backed leather chair that fronted an impressive deep amber, French polished, Victorian desk and though his office was spacious, Elliot's physical size made it seem small. Indeed, his chubby face and overall physical bulk appeared to fill the room. He smoked small cheroots and his dark, Saville Row, pin stripped suit's were frequently flecked with the odd trail of ash. He had no sense of embarrassment, his self-esteem was unassailable and he exuded an indestructible confidence. His eyes twinkled as though all that he saw amused him. He was considered to be a maverick even amongst maverick lawyers. His ego extended to infinity, as did his legal intellect, and this made him one of the most successful defence lawyers in the country. He had the reputation of crossing swords with any judge stupid enough to argue with him, and he was seldom bested. He enjoyed turning the tables on any specious logic spouted by a competing lawyer, or a foregone conclusion as far as a court or jury verdict was concerned. It was said that had he the devil for a client, the angels in heaven would desert and surrender paradise.

Now he sat in front of his latest client, one Edmund Lincoln who leaned forward in his chair with an air of determination.

"Mr. Elliot, I'm sure you know why I'm consulting you; you have my solicitors notes and you are already aware of the case I'm sure. It's has been reported nationwide by the media and even you must be of the opinion that there is something fundamentally wrong with what has happened. I'm bemused, concerned and appalled by the treatment bestowed on my employees."

Elliot smiled "Hard to miss it Mr. Lincoln, and yes, I'm sure it all seems rather bizarre to the laymen."

"Not bizarre Mr. Elliot, bloody wrong. Not to be given bail, to in effect having to endure a prison sentence – by that I mean the time between arrest and the next court appearance which will be very many weeks away – to know, as everyone does, that your so called crime was in self-defence, that the CPS insisted on a prosecution purely to absolve themselves from being seen as negligent of partisan. Isn't that wrong, where's the justice in that? The bloody CPS don't have to go through what my people will have to go through, and yet not a single lawyer or any part of the judiciary has spoken out. To most people the so called criminal justice system – if that is what it is – stinks."

Elliot gave a sympathetic smile.

"Yes, over all it is unfair – but what might be more unfair would be if the CPS chose to set themselves up as judge and jury. How do you think the relatives of the dead man would react if the CPS simply waved a white flag and ignored what could be a case of unlawful homicide?"

He gave a resentful exclamation.

"Huh – relatives? From what I understand, from reports in the newspapers the man had few relatives, only victims, lots of them! He had a criminal record as long as your arm. Okay he had severe psychological problems – insidious paranoia with Schizophrenia it is said – but that doesn't detract from the fact that he attacked first."

He waited for Elliot's response but it wasn't what he wanted to hear.

"Come now Mr. Lincoln, are you trying the case before we get to it? It's not me, or come to that anyone else prepared to listen to you, who will need to be convinced. You see, until this matter is tested in open court everyone with an interest in the matter will have his or her own interpretation on what happened. Giving your people a 'no case to answer' from the CPS would leave a bad taste in a lot of peoples mouths. Let me remind you of the old adage – justice must not only be done, it must be seen to be done!"

"Exactly my point," he snapped back, "so far there is no sign of this 'justice' you speak about being done – due process yes, but it has nothing to do with justice. As I understood it the legal definition of justice is that everyone gets treated fairly. Yet here is a case where the CPS force everyone though the mill just so they can show clean hands. They don't care what the cost is, financial or emotional, to the individuals involved or those around them. They make everyone else pay so that they can be free of criticism. They behave as though they do not have discretion, and yet umpteen cases demonstrate otherwise. It's only when they face a potential scandal, or public criticism, that they hide behind due process."

Elliot gave a shrug of his shoulders.

"Agreed – may I say you missed your vocation Mr. Elliot – you should have been a lawyer. Yes, it's a very flawed system but it's the best we've got and for now we have to live with it. Incidentally, I've read the notes from your solicitor and seen a copy of the security video, I'm fairly certain that your employees will not face a conviction. Indeed, I'd bet on it. However, that said, it should not be a case of walking into this with our eyes shut. If you wish me to act for your employees I will want every fact that leans in their favour – in short I will take no chances. I will treat this case as though each one of your employees was caught holding a smoking gun. In short, we assume it's going to be tough and we take no chances. Do we agree?"

He nodded, "Yes Mr. Elliot, I would very much like to retain you to defend my people – I trust you are their best hope of an acquittal."

"Good," he replied, "make an appointment with my secretary for both of us to visit the remand centre – she'll confirm a date. We need to talk to our er' victims!"

The journey back home from London was by tube and train. He read all the newspaper articles and their editorials. On the whole they supported his point of view, some calling for a revision of the way the CPS worked. Nevertheless, a great deal of legal interest supported the principle of proper examination of the facts – in the presence of a judge and jury.

It gave him time to consider everything that might result, or be a consequence of the present debacle. He pondered for a moment on the irony thrown up by the depressing fiasco he had to grapple with.

Certainly money was a factor and not one newspaper mentioned the financial and emotional penalties of being at the wrong end of 'due process'. Elliot and the associated legal costs were going to be horrendous but that at least he could cater for – it would be tight, but the shop takings in recent times and his own reserves would meet it.

A good deal of the money he could throw at legal support for his people had come from the insurance settlement paid out after Carol's death. Sadly it was ironic that in life she dreaded the loss of the business, yet in death she was possibly its salvation.

As the train sped past Guildford station he felt a twinge of regret that the best laid plans he had recently made were now never to see the light of day – the Guildford shop would undoubtedly be in other hands by now. And yet...had he signed the lease there would have been little chance of finding all the resource necessary to back Mark, Sam and Peter. Maybe his guardian angel had contrived his being unable to make a decision that day – maybe!

As he alighted from the train, seeing his familiar home station, he suddenly realised that he had put himself into a difficult situation.

His people were being held at Hillsview remand centre near Swindon and his intention of seeing them with Elliot in tow could be compromised. He wanted to see them prior to any appearance by Elliot. There were other things to say and he had no intention of delaying a visit just because Elliot had a well-filled diary.

He phoned Hillsview the next day and after four aborted attempts he eventually got through enabling him to request a visit. He was then told to wait until the prisoners could confirm they wanted to see him. He got the okay a few hours later and was given times for the usual three 1 hour visits per week that remand prisoners were usually allowed. He opted for the most immediate opening and was then told that the remand centre's governor was particularly generous when it came to visiting times, but it was not to be abused. He found this admission slightly amusing – why the hell would anyone visiting a prison want to stay on long enough to risk being locked up with the rest?

His appointment was for two days hence and he decided to drive up to the to the centre. In the meantime he needed to ensure the business would continue to limp along in the absence of his key personnel. Once he had organised that aspect he could concentrate on extracting his people from the clutches of the law.

8

Hillsview was less foreboding than he expected, it presented a fairly modern design externally. The buff coloured brickwork and open space behind the security fencing gave it the appearance of large school or college, and were it not for the tight security at the entrance one would imagine it to be an academic establishment of some kind.

Prisoners seemed to be free to engage in pastimes, hobbies and other entertainments. There was no indication of cell doors being constantly locked with prisoners incarcerated for 23 hours each day. He learned that prisoners who were on remand had the privilege of being treated as innocent of any crime, because they were yet to be convicted. As such, they were allowed far more freedom than their fellow inmates who had been convicted and sentenced and were waiting transfer to a closed prison.

The meeting took place in an open, airy room furnished with a large polished wooden table and six chairs. He was shown into the room by a jovial, middle aged warder who clearly enjoyed his standing joke with visitors that 'in the event the person they were visiting didn't turn up in the next ten minutes, they were at liberty to join the prisoners in the canteen for tea and a head count.'

However, the amusing warning went unheeded and no more than two minutes elapsed before the door opened and Mark Stapleford walked in beaming with relief and pleasure.

"Christ Eddy, I'm so glad to see you, we thought we'd been abandoned - only Fiona managed to get any news through to us and that was sketchy."

They sat at the table and as he looked at Mark, now dressed in what appeared to be prison issue overalls, the strain he had endured over the preceding days showed, a pale, drawn face matched to an anxious expression.

"Yeah, sorry Mark I know it's been four days but I needed to be able to give you some critical news before I saw you."

As he said that he realised he had phrased his reply badly – Mark's face dropped.

He held up his hand, palm forward, to deflect Mark's concern.

"God, no! I didn't mean bad news; on the contrary it should be encouraging. I persuaded your solicitor to finalise your case notes quickly and get them to one of the best defence lawyers in the country. He agreed to see me immediately. His name is Nathan Elliot and you'll be meeting him shortly. He's very optimistic about your chances of acquittal so don't despair."

Mark shrugged his shoulders.

"It's not the trial per se we are worried about. What pisses us off is that there is going to be one at all. Peter and Sam are as aggrieved as me; we shouldn't be facing charges in the first place. My protest in refusing to plead at the Magistrates court was I hoped, along with all the spectators' and media pressure, going to bring about some kind of reconsideration – more fool me. Peter and Sam thought the same, but here we bloody well are and we bloody well don't like it."

He gave Mark a sympathetic grin.

"You and ten million others. I've been through this over and over again with those knowledgeable in legalities. They all point to the Crown Prosecution Service refusing to take responsibility for not prosecuting because it will be seen by some as unfair to the those who view this Philip Dighton as a victim, even though I was told that had he lived he would have been charged with grievous bodily harm. You know I suppose that Dighton was short of one kidney, a drug addict, a psychotic and well known to the police. A normal man would have survived your test probe; Dighton was already half dead when you stabbed him. It's ridiculous, but they want a trial so that they can appear impartial and squeaky clean."

Mark simply stared at him, shaking his head slightly in disbelief as he spoke.

"So we've got to go through the bloody mill just to satisfy some sense of decorum - that's it isn't it?"

"In a nutshell, yes."

Mark shook his head more vigorously.

"Okay Eddy, I know we can rely on you. How's the business by the way, and what about money. From your remarks about this Elliot guy he won't be cheap."

"Don't worry about costs Mark, I've catered for whatever it takes to get you freed. As for the business, for the interim I've reorganised things. In between my commitments to you three, I'll be running things. That said, I shall try to see all of you as much as possible. My next visit will be with Mr. Elliot, your brief. I want you, Peter and Sam to set aside your resentment and frustration and do exactly what he says. He's your best hope of an acquittal so we are going to play the game until you walk out of the court exonerated. Afterwards Mark...afterwards I say...is when we go on the offensive and try to stop this stupid process ever happening again. And though it may not be any consolation to you right now, regarding the incident, I think you did the right thing for the right reasons. Okay?"

He saw a change in Marks body language, the perceptible slouch in his body had departed, his face had picked up a flush of colour and now he smiled out of optimism.

"Yes, Eddy - understood. Incidentally how are you feeling? All this must be a strain on you too."

"Forget it, I'm tougher now than before the raid, and I owe you for that."

Mark leaned back in his chair.

"Well, I think we three are going to have to learn patience, one guy I spoke to here has been waiting eleven weeks for his case to come up. If we have as long to wait, our nearest and dearest are going to have as tough a time as us. Not sure how they will survive."

As Mark spoke he realised he had failed to assure him that it was his responsibility to look after the families.

"Don't concern yourself Mark, your Fiona, and those dependent on Peter and Sam, will get the normal housekeeping money. Not sure for how long - but I've organized finances for a twelve week siege, just in case the trial is delayed. I hope that reassures you."

Mark nodded his thanks. "Twelve weeks! I hope to Christ it's not that long. For my Fiona and the others it's the anxiety and worry that's the killer. Still, I'll get to see her fairly often...I hope."

He gave a nod of confirmation remembering Carol and what had killed her.

"I hope it's not that long either Mark - and on that note I will give everyone a lift every time I come up, so you are guaranteed a good few visits."

It was time to move on. He stood up and offered his hand. "Sorry Mark, got to see Peter and Sam yet, and time is pressing. Hang on in Mark, I'll be back to see you all in a few days. *Nil desperandum.*"

The smile he got as Mark exited the room was poignant and again he was deeply saddened that his partner should be treated like this. He promised himself that if it ever came to it again, no bloody crook or petty thief was ever going to cause this much hurt and injustice again.

He met up with Elliot half way to Hillsview in a station car park that allowed him to travel by train for most of the journey up. Elliot was driving a Jaguar F Type, and for all his thick frame and apparent lack of dexterity drove like a Formula 1 driver. He took very little notice of speed limits. When he asked Elliot what he did if he was caught speeding the lawyer simply smiled and said he had every section of the Road Traffic Act committed to memory. He had twice threatened the police through their chief constable with an action for stopping him without reasonable cause and for unlawful interpretation of the RTA. He had only once had to pay a fine and even then only because he was too busy with another court case to counter the allegation or do otherwise.

Over the twenty minutes they were driving together he began to develop an even greater respect for the man who was going to defend his people. Elliot had a charming and in some respects modest way about him. He made no effort to demonstrate a superior intellect or to show how forceful he could be. If anything, it seemed to be a case of friendly persuasion rather than an irresistible force.

On arrival at Hillsview it was clear Elliot had prior experience of attending the remand centre. Most of the staff they met recognised him at once and he was on good terms with all of them. It may have been the fact that once he was representing an inmate, it was almost certain that the accused would not be returning to the remand centre after his trial – Elliot seldom failed to convince the courts that his clients were better out of prison than in. No doubt every time Elliot won a case the remand centre staff would cheer, there being one less inmate to worry about.

They were shown into the same room where he had met Mark Stapleford, this time five chairs were occupied instead of the two.

Mark, Sam and Peter had taken the set of chairs opposite the door and as Nathan Elliot was ahead, it was Elliot who introduced himself. He watched fascinated, as Elliot seemed to bond to each man the moment his hands touched theirs. It was almost uncanny, a kind of voodoo of the empathetic kind.

He said nothing, ensuring that he didn't break the spell or do something that would make Elliot's aura the less.

The big lawyer settled into a chair and without embarrassment flicked a small trail of ash off of his grey-stripped suit. He then looked up and caught the eye of the three silent men at his front.

"Gentlemen, I'm certain that you see your forthcoming trial as an opportunity to embarrass and humiliate the criminal justice system. If I'm correct, I would tend to sympathise with your attitude; as do most of the population of this country, and most certainly the media who have raised a storm of protest over your incarceration. Nevertheless, let me disabuse you of your approach and objectives. First, what you wish for cannot be done without an acquittal at your trial. Second, we have no certainty of an acquittal. I say that because for all your massive national support I guarantee I could find twelve men or women who, making up a jury, would convict you at the drop of a hat. Why? Because there are those who cherish the rule of law more than they cherish what you and I might call right thinking and justice.

To them the law is sacrosanct and no one must be allowed to slip past its rulings."

As Elliot spoke he scrutinized his three men who were now beginning to look despairingly at the lawyer. Sam in particular, who still carried a facial dressing, lighter than before, but still witness to his own argument for justice.

Then Elliot smiled, fixedly, at all three men.

"Now, I am sure from your crest fallen looks that you are now doubtful that this forthcoming trial can be resolved in your favour. Do not mistake me – I speak as I do to ensure you are aware of the pitfalls, and the fact that verdicts in courts of law are seldom wholly predictable – though in your case I would admit that there is much in your favour. I intend to call only you Mr. Stapleford to give evidence. If your testimony, and the video evidence, does not seem to have the necessary impact – and remember I am watching the jury – then you Mr. Hill will take the stand. In both your cases, I want calmness and dignity. The witness box is not going to be a platform for a tirade or outburst against the system. The more measured and objective your responses the better you will appear. You all have impeccable records as law-abiding citizens – that will be crucial because it will demonstrate you were forced by extreme circumstances to take the action that you did; and it could never be your normal habit. Remember too that you will be cross-examined by counsel for the prosecution and by me – though mine will be focused on demonstrating that the charges against you are invalid. Again, I caution you against allowing your bile to rise and subsequently expressing anger with the prosecution's claims, implications or innuendos. I will intervene where and when I can in order to deflect disingenuous prosecution queries and claims which could result in indignation on your part. Remember – calmness and dignity will win this."

As he paused, Elliot tapped his top pocket, absent-mindedly looking for his cheroots. He then lifted a hand with his finger pointed skywards.

"One other thing my friends, you might be tempted to influence the outcome of all this by leaking the odd personal opinion to the outside world. Don't! The media are better left to their own devices. You will find that having once allowed a comment or two of yours to leak out, you will find it thrown back at you with venom by the prosecution – it's dangerous, don't do it! Now any questions?"

The three looked at each other somewhat stunned by what had been said but finally all three mumbled a reply in the negative.

Elliot gave them a warm smile. "Very well, I'm glad at least to have three intelligent clients and I look forward to seeing you all again prior to the hearing. If anything occurs to you, or you need advice please convey it through Mr. Lincoln here – I am at your disposal. Have faith gentlemen, I trust your stay here will not be too long or too fraught."

Elliot pulled himself awkwardly off of his chair and shook hands with each man.

He too in turn took their hands as they filed past him and he gave each of them his assurance that he would be returning shortly and that they would be kept constantly in touch with family and events.

Mark Stapleford, the last to file out, stopped abreast of him.

"We'll follow the party line Eddy but we won't be silent when this is all over. As you said, afterwards is when we make our stand and complaints. Assuming we are all set free, we are going to change this bloody business – just you wait!"

Mark turned and walked out of the door followed by a warder.

As the three disappeared Nathan Elliot pursed his lips.

"I would like to think I know how they feel but my feelings can't be anything like as keen and as biting as it is for those three. Come Mr. Lincoln, we should not be maudlin. I know where to get some excellent pub food – it's a about fifteen miles down the road – allow me to invite you to lunch."

9

As it was it took six weeks to get to trial. In more than one way he was immensely grateful that it had. It meant less frustration for his people, less for their families and a definite surplus in the war chest. He had seen the effect the tension was having on everyone, not least himself, and it was a welcome respite to know that at last the litigation would come to a conclusion.

As the day dawned for the hearing he looked back on all that had been done to help his people – he had been determined not to let anyone directly associated with those in prison feel they had been left to flounder. He had worked hard to keep the business energetic and functioning, but not failing to find the time to see family members, pay subsistence and at the same time periodically visit the remand centre; either alone or with those wanting to see the three prisoners.

As he sat in the courtroom's public gallery he watched as the available seats filled up. It was large by modern standards and could accommodate a very large public viewing, but in the present circumstances it would have had to have been a football stadium to provide room for all those thousands wanting attendance. Indeed, he had arrived very early, knowing that the case was going to attract a massive audience and not wanting to have to stand or be refused entry.

Nathan Elliot had told him not to expect a discussion on the day of the trial - he was going to be too busy with last minute instructions for the three accused. Elliot had, however, assured him that he was not only 'confident' but 'looking forward to a good poke at the prosecution'; the prosecution case to be presented by one Richard Lister QC, an old adversary of Elliot's. He looked at the large screen that had been erected to the side of the jury's gallery knowing that in the last analysis the video of the incident would be decisive in any verdict.

As the already sworn jury lined up, he seemed to lose his sense of optimism – he was aware of how fickle fate was and he wished he had a contingency plan to rely on in the event the case was lost. As counsel – Elliot, his pupils, and the prosecution gaggle appeared – he desperately wanted to run down and plead with Elliot to guarantee the verdict he wanted – but this was fantasy and he dismissed the thought as it appeared.

The judge, a somewhat athletic and well-groomed Mr. Justice Andrews, came to the bench in a flourish and his red robe was literally a ball of fire. He almost immediately brought the court to order and as he ordered the accused to be brought up from the cells a hush descended on the now filled to capacity courtroom. Except for the odd cough the enveloping silence took on an almost ominous feel. When asked to confirm their identities and plead, each of the three spoke strongly and in keeping with their instructions from Elliot replied 'Not Guilty'.

The two QC's, perfectly groomed in black gowns white collarettes and wigs, lent an air of authority to the proceedings, though each stood at ease in the now strained quite of the courtroom. The judge carried out the usual courtesies of welcoming the two senior counsel; both of whom were obviously familiar to him, and then addressed the courtroom.

"I am fully aware of the disturbances that took place previously when the accused were brought before the magistrates for commitment. Though I accept that some may believe it was warranted, that kind of behaviour will not happen today or here! Should there be any disruption of the proceedings about to take place in this court, I will clear the court and this trial will take place in camera. I trust I am understood."

The judge stared into the courtroom, meeting only a brooding silence as he surveyed the packed seating and galleries. With a grunt of satisfaction he turned to counsel.

"I take you will lead Mr. Lister."

Lister stood. "I will My Lord."

Lister had a proud bearing and a tangible presence; he was tall and used a carefully modulated, well articulated, voice – gentle yet penetrating.

"My Lord, it is central to this country's criminal justice system that unlawful acts are tried in open court to establish the veracity of the allegation that the act is unlawful. Is the charge valid – is the charge appropriate – is there truly a breach of the law? The purpose of a court such as this is to fairly and openly consider such matters. This hearing is intended to examine the charges raised against the accused and to ensure that the processing of that examination is transparent and impartial. In no way should the weighing of the relevant facts be obfuscated by factors or events that play no part in the interpretation of the law surrounding the alleged transgression. It is this that makes this case extraordinary, in that the accused are in one instance facing a charge of unlawful killing and in two other instances of aiding and abetting that killing. It is manifestly obvious to all that there is no defence in law to killing a person other than that of self-defence, and even then it is necessary to demonstrate that it was unavoidable. This being so, and as I have implied, we come to the extraordinary aspects of this case, all of which will be revealed in detail in due course, but in essence can be said to involve and to revolve around mistaken perceptions coupled to aggressive reactions none of which were warranted and were needlessly violent. My Lord, Philip David Dighton was killed as he attempted to return a pair of faulty earphones to the shop where he purchased them. In being unfairly accosted by sales staff in the shop where he intended to return the earphones, he took defensive action by retrieving a knife from his pocket and using it to ward off the attack. The knife was a recent purchase for his mother's kitchen and had been bought at her request only ten minutes prior to being attacked. He did not normally go about his business armed with a knife. As he fought back he was then confronted by one of the accused carrying an electrical test probe, a needle ended instrument some seven inches long. As the confrontation continued the defendant drove this probe deep into Dighton's lower torso and Mr. Dighton subsequently collapsed. Although Mr. Dighton was removed to hospital he was pronounced dead on arrival. It appears that having at one time had his left kidney removed because of a tumour, and the other weakened by his lifestyle, the damage caused by the probe caused renal failure and it was fatal.

There is a clear video record of the incident and it will be shown to the jury in due course. However, to show it out of context will not ultimately enlighten the jury in their deliberations and I intend to call witnesses to support interpretation of the video evidence – not least because without appropriate authentication of the victim's character, standing and state of mind at the time of his death there would be no explanation as to why the incident took place and the reason why Dighton and the defendants behaved as they did. As such, I call Julia Dighton as my first witness."

He sat, along with any others; listening to Lister paint a very different story to what he and many others thought was true. It appeared that the appearance of Julia Dighton was intended to add to the distortion.

As she was sworn in she was already in tears. Lister's modulated voice addressed her, coaxing out a response.

"Miss Dighton – please tell us about your brother."

And so it went – how disturbed Philip Dighton had become when his father died, how he had fallen into bad company which had exploited his emotional and child like weaknesses, how he had never had a stable job and what few he had held down ending in bad blood between him and his employers. How, destitute and desperate, he had taken part in a series of street muggings and had been arrested. How he had been treated in prison for schizophrenia and had benefited from prescribed medication. Then they had found the tumour on his left kidney, which resulted in surgery and chemotherapy. On release from hospital, and afterwards prison, he had tried to go straight but almost immediately abandoned his treatment. He had then relapsed and had again fallen foul of the law, this time for fighting in a pub causing actual bodily harm. Over the past year he had kept to his medication and had religiously attended his mental health clinics. He seemed to have turned a corner and everyone was proud of him for trying so hard."

"What about the knife Miss Dighton, why was he carrying a knife?"

"My mother mentioned that she needed a new kitchen knife before Philip left with his earphones, but I don't remember her asking him to buy one."

Lister waited for a moment as she closed her tearful recounting of her brother's history. It seemed he was about to ask another question but thought better of it.

Lister sank back onto the bench with a "Your witness."

There was no doubt that Julia Dighton had attracted much in the way of sympathy from the court. Even Elliot delayed cross-examination for a respectful few minutes to allow her to compose herself.

As Nathan Elliot stood up he nodded an acknowledgement to the judge – thanking him for not insisting that he press on and ignore Julia Dighton's distress.

As the courtroom settled back into a sombre silence Elliot smiled at Julia Dighton.

"Miss Dighton – I hope to spare you any more distressing recollections about your brother. I have only one query and I hope you can answer it truthfully. I have here a list of prescriptions issued by you brothers mental health team. As you say, he was definitely prescribed medication for his disorder. However, it appears that the pharmacy where your brother would usually pick up his prescriptions has no record of any collection of his medication for the last six months. Do you remember seeing your brother take any medication prior to his death?"

Julia Dighton took breath and held it, her tears again streaming down over already glistening, wet cheeks. She then slowly shook her head, and with even more tears breaking out from her eyes put her head in her hands and continued to sob.

Elliot signed and said, "No more questions my Lord."

The judge leaned forward. "The witness is excused – please remember Miss Dighton, you are still under oath." With a nod of acknowledgement she was led from the witness box and out of the court.

The second prosecution witness was a psychologist, a strangely and unexpectedly nervous Dr. Litton.

"Dr Litton, Philip Dighton was you patient for how long?" Lister turned an ear to the reply, almost theatrical in its pose.

Litton stuttered slightly before visibly collecting himself with a slight stiffening of his shoulders.

"Well...well, other than a break for his cancer treatment, in all over sixteen months – the first four while he was in prison,"

Lister paused and then, "What was the diagnosis Dr. Litton – in short, what was his mental state when you began treatment?"

Litton delayed his answer, clearly recollecting his memories of Dighton,

"Originally a deep seated psychosis but as his exposure to the psychoanalysis went on, the diagnosis was revised to 'insidious paranoia with schizoid tendencies'. Much of his condition had originated from the appalling events that took place in his childhood. He was a very disturbed personality."

Lister nodded strongly as if to emphasis Litton's comment.

"This mental disturbance, how did it manifest itself?"

"He was threat sensitive in the extreme – he often saw danger and threat where there was none. He would become deeply suspicious of the most innocent events. In short, it was a clear case of deep-seated paranoia. However, that said, it did not always manifest itself as a typical reaction to paranoia – that is, a tendency to react fearfully and to become anxious. In Dighton's case it often created a tendency to instantaneous violence against the supposed threat. He would attack what he thought was menacing him even though it was clear there was no real threat. He once recited the old adage to us, 'just because you're paranoid doesn't mean they aren't out to get you'. And yes, he often mocked or parodied his own paranoia. However, the schizophrenia was another matter. He was a positive schizophrenic – that is, delusional – thereby exaggerating his paranoia."

"Did medication help?"

"Yes, antipsychotic drugs helped significantly. Aropiprazole and Clozapine seemed to suit him and most of his symptoms appeared to abate."

Lister paused, a finger raised in contemplation.

"Dr. Litton, how would Philip Dighton have behaved after neglecting his medication?"

"He would have reverted to his usual psychosis – perhaps more seriously."

"Thank you Dr. Litton. Your witness," Lister said. He then gave a curt bow to Litton and sat down.

Elliot rose smoothly from his bench and then lent down to say something to Lister who gave an agreeable nod. Elliot then faced Litton.

"Dr. Litton, thank you for your clear and lucid cover of Philip Dighton's psychological state. Tell the court please, how do you think he would have reacted to being physically accosted by two strangers in a shop? What would trigger the response of pulling out a knife and severely wounding one of the two?"

Litton smiled, "As I said, he could, and usually would, react violently to a real or a perceived threat. Given his condition, and without medication, any other response would have been unlikely."

Elliot smiled, "Thank you Dr. Litton, No other questions."

As the judge dismissed Litton with the usual warning, Elliot turned away from the front bench and looked at the court gallery. As he caught Elliot's eye he saw a slight raising of Elliot's eyebrows.

It suddenly dawned on him what was going on.

Was he now the only one that realised that Lister and Elliot were working together, that so far all the evidence was in favour of the accused, that Philip Dighton had been clearly characterised as an unstable, unpredictable and very dangerous person who could not be relied on to behave sensibly. No matter his intention to change his earphones in a civilised way, any slight disturbance was prone to make him violent.

As this dawned on him it obviously also registered with the three men in the dock. Mark Stapleford, Peter Lansdale and Sam Hill turned to look in the direction Elliot had signalled and when they saw who the raised eyebrows had been aimed at, they gave out broad smiles.

As Elliot turned away, Lister addressed the jury.

"Members of the jury, what you are about to see is the security video taken inside the Lincoln shop on the day Philip Dighton died. I would ask you to give it your full attention. Likewise, at the completion of the showing you are at liberty to ask for it to be shown again, or for you to ask questions that may arise from your viewing. I am sure my Lord the judge will assist you in any queries arising out of the law regarding this matter."

Lister gave a short bow to the judge and then pressed a button on a remote control.

10

The video was a silent capture of the events on that fateful day and was viewed in absolute silence by all those watching. As the fatal blow from Mark's probe was driven home the audience remained mute but the previous slashing arc of Dighton's blade, and the huge gush of blood from the six inch wound on Sam Hill's face, brought cries of disbelief from some in the courtroom. Not even Sam's furious response at being badly injured failed to invoke any sign of displeasure from the crowd. As the pictures showed Dighton collapsing to the ground, with the three defenders standing around him and then trying to revive him, there appeared to be no expressions of sympathy from the public. On the contrary – not a sound accompanied his final moments on camera as he was carried into the ambulance.

As the video ended the courtroom filled with a buzzing exchange of opinion, but so far as the jury were concerned they needed no re-showing of the incident.

Leaning to his left, the foreman took comments passed on juror to juror along the seated members. As the hubbub in the courtroom began to subside the foreman stood up and attempted to get himself heard. .

"My Lord – My Lord...the jury wishes to know if it can bring in a verdict prior to counsel completing their closing arguments?"

Justice Andrews looked shocked and for the moment said nothing. As he considered the foreman's question the gathering immediately realised that something rare and unorthodox was taking place and a hush descended on the proceedings.

"It is contrary to protocol and, as far as I know, has no precedent in law or custom so I cannot approve of the jury's intention implicit in your query."

The foreman remained standing.

"My Lord, we are of one mind on this – whatever the length of the proceedings in this case, this jury will bring in a unanimous verdict which is already decided. Regardless of what transpires from now on, it will not change our decision. In the interests of justice, cost and pragmatism, there is no point in allowing this case to continue."

As this was said Justice Andrews gave an indignant gasp.

"You, and your fellow jurors were instructed not discuss this matter outside the jury room, only there are you entitled to review and confer on all aspects of the case. You are reminded that you can bring in a verdict of guilty or not guilty – that is your prerogative. "

You have yet to hear all the evidence, I cannot see how you could possible decide a unanimous verdict *a priori* and without discussion.

The foreman remained unmoved by the retort.

"Nevertheless My Lord, we have, and we find the charges against these men ludicrous. The need for us to debate the appropriateness of guilty or not guilty is superfluous. The inclusion of guilty in any consideration we might make is specious – Regardless of the options therefore, we will not convict."

As this was said a number of jurors nodded their heads in agreement. It was an unmistakable confirmation and the courtroom erupted. A voice over-rang the hubbub, "Let's hear some justice for a change!"

Justice Andrews looked at the source of the voice with a sullen, resentful gaze. His response of "Silence – I say silence in court." was only just audible.

He sat as dumbstruck as many of those sitting around him. It was clear that the three in the dock had been effectively exonerated – nothing that came afterwards could change the fact that a jury had chosen to ignore the letter of the law and had decided in line with what most right thinking people thought was fair. Even a mistrial could not change that, and a retrial would undoubtedly produce the same result.

Justice Andrews now sat motionless looking at the jury with disdain. Then, he turned to the courtroom and beckoned to Elliot and Lister. Both counsel moved up to the bench and with both leaning towards the judge in order to be heard began an intense exchange. This however lasted for no more than a minute. As Lister and Elliot turned away from the bench Andrews addressed the court.

In a grating voice and clearly indignant at the turn of events Andrews rasped, "I am minded to dismiss the jury for miscon-duct...which I do. On further consideration I find sufficient grounds for a mistrial. The jury is dismissed and in the interests of justice the defendants are free to go."

Without further pause Andrews hurried from the rostrum and disappeared from view. He may well have heard the uproar that his decision created, certainly it was a well-received judgment and those close to the defendants were delirious with joy.

As he felt a warm glow of pleasure and relief course through him, he realised that now he – and his people – could get back to normality. The nightmare, so it appeared, was virtually at an end.

Outside the courtroom the chaotic crush of people made his wait for familiar faces an impatient but pleasurable ordeal. He tried to keep his place while throngs of others lingered in the hallway to congratulate or interview the three defendants. However, the first to appear from the court entrance was Nathan Elliot and Richard Lister. Still with their robes on they were in deep conversation, a conversation that elicited mutually broad smiles from both. It was obvious that their discussion was on a very genial basis.

As they came abreast of him Nathan Elliot's face lit up with recognition.

"Ah! Lincoln, may I introduce Richard Lister, no doubt you thought him an advocate on behalf of hell, but let me assure you that he is no devil in disguise, quite the contrary."

He shook hands with Lister whose appearance and demeanour was that of someone who had won a case rather than having it taken from him.

"Pleased to meet you Mr. Lincoln, very glad your people are now able to resume their lives – I wish you and them all good fortune." Lister broke free from the handshake and with another smile to Elliot walked away, ignoring those trying to get a statement from him about the lost trial.

He turned back to his smiling advocate. "Well, Mr. Elliot, your optimistic prediction has been confirmed and justified, for which many thanks. I must admit, there were times during the preliminary cross examinations when I thought the strategy was the inverse of what I thought would, or should, take place. It even occurred to me that you and Mr. Lister had exchanged roles. Did I read things mistakenly? If I hadn't know better, I would have concluded that you and he had joined forces."

Elliot smiled and turned towards the court entrance as if expecting an arrival. As he did so he pointed and gave a 'come on' wave of his hand.

Turning in the same direction he was overjoyed to see Mark Stapleford and his two 'accomplices' besieged by reporters and family at the court entrance. Their appearance caused a surge of people to brush past Elliot and himself and quite soon the original horde of spectators no longer surrounded them.

As they became isolated from the many ears in proximity to them, Elliot came closer creating a more intimate discussion.

"The thing is Lincoln, even the CPS were embarrassed by the rumpus this case started, but you know the ways of bureaucracy, they can't be seen to retreat on something like this. Lister's brief was to concede the case surreptitiously – he had no intention of creating a public scandal by pinning your people to the wall. Prior to the trial we had a little heart–to–heart and decided that in the context of both our instructions, we would make it impossible for any sane jury to convict your three friends. In terms of that *sic transit gloria mundi*."

"But what about the judge, he seemed very displeased."

Elliot gave a huge grin, "Oh, he'll await the CPS to call for another trial – but he won't get it. The CPS will be pleased to see the back of this – no longer in the public interest you see. As for the judge, he has the distinction of presiding over one of the most bizarre trials of the century. He will be lauded and applauded by all his bewigged peers. Believe me, he'll revel in it. As for you and your friends, you have nothing further to worry about – ah, that said, here they come."

Elliot had turned to welcome the appearance of the three defendants. Each had the elated look and a facial blush that only those given a reprieve from a terrible fate could contrive. Behind them joyous friends and relatives were babbling with glee.

As the three approached, they advanced first towards Elliot and started pumping his hand in grateful thanks – it was clear that they too had surmised that in all probability the case had been rigged in their favour.

It was Sam Hill who having thanked Elliot then came forward and gave his employer a beaming smile.

"Hello boss – can't tell you how grateful we are. How you swung it is a miracle. We'll never forget it."

He looked at Sam's face; a face now somewhat less obscured by dressings. Part of an angry looking weal of a healing wound peeped out from the lower edge of the dressing, but this was a much lighter dressing than the one seen earlier.

"How you feeling Sam – face okay?"

"Oh sure – I'm on the mend. They over dressed it before to attract some sympathy from the jury. Not needed now!"

He smiled, Elliot had thought of everything – talk about contingency plans.

Now Mark and Peter had said their goodbyes to Elliot who strode off with a cheerful wave of his hand.

He hugged each man, not knowing what to say but almost brought to tears by the emotional aura of the moment.

"Hello boys – how's it feel – do we celebrate or is it home first?"

Each smiling face took on an indecisive but happy look.

Mark Stapleford responded first.

"Well, we've said goodbye to the prison overalls. I think I'm dressed for a short celebration. How about it?"

The other two nodded their consent and he started to usher all three towards the courthouse exit. He then remembered all the others and waved the gaggle of thrilled supporters forward.

"Come on – drinks are on me!"

Without any need for further encouragement the twelve odd followers behind started to catch up. As they began to move up he thought how wonderful it was going to be to get back to a predictable life.

"Just one thing you three, it's Thursday today. I'm giving you tomorrow off – compassionate leave – you'll have the weekend too of course. However, I expect to see you all in the shop first thing Monday morning – no excuses. Understood?"

They all turned, with delight on their faces and with exclamations of amused uncertainty.

"He laughed back, repeating his instructions and knowing full well that his team would not let him down.

"By the way – Nathan Elliot seemed to get all your attention back then – what was he so pleased about, or is it obvious?"

Mark turned. "In the cells this morning he bet us a thousand pounds each that we would be free by 11 a.m. You may have noticed that we didn't get discharged until 11.35 a.m. He lost!"

Hearing this, he shook his head in total disbelief. Had the last few hours not been so trying he would have been highly amused by the revelation, but given the size of his legal bill it was an ironic twist that a not insignificant proportion of the bill was going to go directly into his employee's and partner's hands. Yet, their ordeal deserved some kind of compensation so he wasn't going to quibble. Be thankful for small mercies, he thought – in this life, it's all you get!

11

It had only been a month since the trial and now all public and media interest in the episode had faded having been replaced by other events. At first his three 'musketeers' had been inundated with requests for interviews and personal stories regarding their experiences, but in every case that had declined – even when a very large fee for an exclusive article was on offer. In this he was not only thankful – he wanted no resurrection of the unhappy event – but admiring of his people for their absolute refusal to take a selfish and mercenary attitude to the enticements. It was clear that they had no wish to wallow in, or capitalise on, an experience so horrific and traumatic that it had cost a life and nearly cost them their freedom.

Other than the fading memory of the trial and its associated furore, the renewal of day-to-day routines for all concerned made for a therapeutic and comforting existence. Trade was good, if not better than the period before the arrests. Some of it may have been elicited by curiosity; some people wanted to see where the well-publicised incident took place, and to catch a glimpse of the 'victims'. Nevertheless, in general they were moving a lot of stock and everyone felt very optimistic about the future. Even he was starting to think about expanding again. He knew the Guildford premises were now out of reach but he also knew that with sufficient effort he could track down something equally as good elsewhere. That, he decided, he would arrange in the next few weeks. For now he had a backlog of paperwork, stock renewals and financial adjustments to worry about – not least the unexpected draining of the reserves over the last few months. Fortunately the cost of all his recent commitments, legal and domestic, had not been as draining and debilitating as he had originally dreaded, so Lincoln and Stapleford were still solvent.

When that thought came to mind, he realised he needed to make a note for the sign-writers to come and fit the new shop sign as soon as possible. He had ordered the new sign just after the arrests, hoping it might be an encouragement to Mark and the others to endure their captivity; but the turmoil of events and his busy schedule had caused it to slip from his mind. It gave him some pleasure to think that Mark would now be here to see the new sign erected.

He scanned the surface of his desk noting the pile of unopened junk mail and sundry correspondence. It had been neglected for some time and he was loath to try and catch up. It was unlikely that anything crucial was contained in it and so he decided to ask Janice to sort it into the relevant ABC categories – 'action', 'bin' or 'consider'. It was usual for most of the mail to end up in category two and was thus consigned to the waste bin.

He called Janice into his office and at the same time decided to have a look at the shop and the new display areas. After that it was a visit to the listening studio to get a hearing of a new set up, enabling three newly launched amplifiers to be heard with any combination of loudspeakers.

He was at the door of his office as Janice knocked. He let her open the door and as she slipped in he pointed to his desk.

"Jan' take that pile of correspondence and sort it out for me please – you know the drill, ABC, put the urgent ones on my desk and I'll attend to them later. Okay?"

She nodded her acceptance.

"How are you by the way – pleased that everything has settled down? What's this about you getting married soon – will I be invited to dance at your wedding?"

Janice blushed, "I'm am getting engaged Mr. Lincoln. My fiancé is trying to placate our families – it's difficult."

She turned away, hoping not to have to explain the 'difficulties'.

He smiled as he let the office door come open, "I'll keep my fingers crossed for you dear. Try to get that mail done as soon as possible, I'll be back later on."

As he closed the door he looked about him surveying the whole of the shops audio display and components racking. There were three customers to his left in the music and instruments section while another two were deep in conversation with Peter Lansdale. Sam Hill was concentrating on some paper work behind the centre counsel with its glass-fronted showcase of earphones, vinyl pick-ups and sundry supplementary devices for CD and vinyl playback.

Of Mark Stapleford there was no sign but that was to be expected; as usual he was ensconced in the workshop no doubt revelling in fault finding a fifty-year-old amplifier. His partner had amazing abilities, but in the end always reverted to his one love – making something work better than it had originally. But that of course was it! If it were broken, even when it was a business, Mark would move heaven and earth to make it work again, only better than before. And by God, he had!

As the outside weather – overcast skies, blustery showers and squally rain – darkened the interior of the shop, he reviewed what needed to be done to ensure the future of the business. However, whatever needed to be done would not be done today. As he looked out, the bad weather was beginning to worsen and it was less than ideal for hunting new premises; or for looking at what equipment was being sold by competing outlets. In short, he was confined to the shop for the rest of the day.

A little disappointed he turned about, intent on returning to his office. At that moment Mark Stapleford appeared at the workshop door staring at a piece of paper.

"Eddy, a word please."

He stopped and let Mark catch him up.

"Problem?"

Mark looked worried.

"Yeah – can we go into your office?"

He opened his door and allowed Mark to precede him. As the door closed behind them Mark turned and proffered the paper he was reading.

"Bloody bastard insurance company Eddy, they have withdrawn cover!"

"What? Why? How is it – I mean, why are they telling you?"

The news was a blow – and the need for Mark to notify him instead of the other way around was also a shock.

"I arranged the insurance Eddy – remember? At the time you were in no shape to arrange anything."

Suddenly embarrassed by the reminder that he had been effectively out of his mind for a time, he changed tack.

"Yeah, okay – understood. But on what grounds – why now?"

I suggest you read the first paragraph – there's no ambiguity in what they say."

He looked down at the letter and started to read.

'We regret that in the light of your employees recent court case, and in consideration of the risk to your insurers of another similar incident likely to invite a claim – either under your public liability or legal support clauses – we must now give you notice that subject to the conditions of your policy (under section 2 paragraph 1), we are terminating your

cover with immediate effect. This will not affect any retrospective claim made while the policy was in force, and any premiums paid in advance of this notice will be refunded.'

It was devastating news, he read it again but the words conveyed the same shock as the first time.

"Christ Mark – what's this section 2 nonsense?"

"The insurance company insisted on a get out clause if they considered that the estimated risk at the time of issuing the policy had later become unacceptably greater. Yes, it stinks Eddy – but it was the best I could get at the time."

He held on to the letter with a tight grip, as though he could get his hands round the neck of the author.

"This leaves us bloody vulnerable Mark – is there no alternative, no other insurance company that will cover us?"

"Well, I can give it another try – see if anything has changed since the last search for cover. Maybe the brokers can come up with something new, we've nothing to lose – but in truth I have my doubts we'll get anything like the kind of cover we need."

He returned the letter to Mark who folded it long ways and slipped it into the breast pocket of his shirt.

"I'll leave it with you Mark – do what you can."

Mark nodded and turned on his heel, as he did so he hesitated and turned about again.

"Eddy, we have to be pragmatic – if we can't get any insurance we are in real trouble, particularly in terms of public liability, recovery of stock and destruction of housing and premises, not to mention legal support.

When the insurance was being negotiated and the brokers were hitting a brick wall, I was forced to consider what options we had if no one would actually insure us. I could only come up with one solution – make the premises a trap for any would be raiders. Yes,

I know that would not make any difference to things like public liability or legal support but let's face it, most of the insurance we have paid for is so remote a possibility for a claim on the insurers that it hardly matters. The policy that has just been rescinded provided the minimum cover. As you now it was so basic it had no legal, accidental theft or earnings cover – in short, damn near useless. Our main concern, and always has been, is what happens if we get another ram raid or something like it. Just think, if we could ensure that anyone breaking in was going to escape empty handed without us losing too much in terms of stock or repairs, we would not need to pay exorbitant premiums to some bloody greedy insurance outfit. By saving the massive premiums we are paying now, a few months would see us with sufficient money in the kitty to pay for a lot of what the bloody insurance company would grudgingly pay out anyway. See my point?"

He listened with growing interest. Mark was right, if what was being paid out now was allowed to accumulate it would soon amount to a substantial war chest. In effect they would be insuring themselves. The conventional alternative, as it stood, was untenable anyway.

"Okay – I hear you Mark, but how are we to ensure we disrupt, interrupt or limit the damage of a raid. What are you proposing?"

Mark smiled. "That's only a germ of an idea at the moment Eddy, but one I think will work. Give me a day or two and I think I can convince you it's viable."

He looked at his partner and offered a nod of approval.

"Okay Mark – let me know when you are ready. Given the immediate loss of our insurance we had better move fast - I don't want to invite Murphy's Law into our troubles. If your idea is practicable then it needs to be installed yesterday – you know what I mean."

"I do, I'll get it set up for a demonstration this p.m."

Mark flared into life and was out of the office door at a pace.

As Mark closed the door behind him he gave thanks again for such a forthright and sensible partner – never say die was a rare motto these days but Mark Stapleford had it engrained into his psyche. God alone knew what he would have done if he had no Mark to rely on. He was looking forward to what Mark had planned – he could guarantee it was going to be amazing.

12

The empty workshop retained its characteristic smell – hot plastics, solder resin and whatever it was the manufacturers sprayed onto electronic printed circuit boards. Now, with all of the engineers absent on their lunch break, he wondered slowly around the extensive cluster of workbenches and racks of equipment. The benches were covered in dismantled amplifiers, CD units under test, scattered electronic components and tools, and each bench had its individual set of test instruments. His admiration for those able to do this kind of work escalated.

He felt a little regretful that his own electronics knowledge was meagre and a slight sense of shame kept him away from the experts who worked for him. Mark however never made him feel inferior or second-rate. Perhaps because though he had no insight into circuitry he did at least have a good set of ears and an extremely broad knowledge about what made a good hi-fi set-up.

Now, as he moved between the benches, he began to feel a sense of foreboding – as though there was something irritating his mind that he could not identify or grasp. It was – what was it? And why was he asking the question? Looking around his vision started to blur slightly and there was the increasing onset of a feeling – that everything was lost, futile and ominous. As these feelings strengthened, he tried to rationalise what he was experiencing – was it post traumatic stress, food poisoning, flu coming on or a mini-stroke?

Whatever it was, it was frightening.

It refused to abate and he began to feel nauseas, dizzy and a desperate need to escape what was happening. Holding on to the edges of successive benches, he managed to make the workshop door. He started to retch and only after an agonising time with inept fingers fumbling with the handle, did he make it into the showroom floor space with the workshop door slammed shut behind him.

He arrived in his office, having staggered and retched his way across the ten yards from the workshop to his office door. With a supreme effort to control his spinning head, heaving stomach and lumbering, unsteady legs, he collapsed into his desk chair.

He only started to recover after some ten minutes of sickening symptoms and thanked his stars for what seemed a miraculous return to normality. It was strange and very worrying – he had hardly ever considered his health as anything else but robust, but what had just happened concentrated his mind wonderfully. Tomorrow he would see his GP and get himself checked out.

His hand reached for a small stack of fliers and promotional leaflets covering new equipment releases by various manufacturers. He always expected to stock the very latest and the very best products, but it took careful appraisal – there was a limit to what brands he could sell and those that were going to sell.

He had started to make notes on each new item when he heard a soft knock. Mark put his head around the door.

"Eddy, were you in the workshop over lunch?"

"Er, yes, how do you know? Did I upset anything? I was only doing my rounds so to speak – getting an idea of what was going on in there."

"It's okay – Maureen saw you. Tell me, did you stay in there long?"

"No, actually only a very short time. I...it was strange I started to feel very ill. I wasn't able to stay in there – I can't explain it, I had to get out. I feel much better now."

Mark smiled and entered the office.

"Glad to hear it Eddy, or my first demonstration would have been a complete flop."

"What do you mean?"

Mark sat down in front of him.

"You pre-empted my demonstration – in fact you tested it for us."

"I don't understand, are you saying...my God, your anti-intruder idea, was that what I experienced?"

Mark offered a look of glee.

"You did, and from what you say it's highly effective. Come on I'll show you."

Mark's two minions Robert and David were standing around the centre workbench looking at a small circuit board. It was relatively insignificant compared to most of the circuit boards he normally saw on the bench surfaces when they were fault finding.

"Hello boys. Robert, tell Mr. Lincoln what we have here."

Robert, still favouring conventional trousers, a navy blue sweater and an open neck shirt pointed a finger at the small circuit board.

"Signal generator Mr. Lincoln – produces a very high frequency signal – twenty one thousand seven hundred and thirty nine cycles per second. To your ears and brain it's not directly detectable as a sound but it still registers as a discord note. The thing is that your brain has a lookup table of sounds it recognizes, but at this level it hears it – that is, it detects it – but can't define it. It's not in the look-up table so to speak. This has a profound physiological and psychological effect. Disorientation, nausea, loss of visual focus and so on, it makes you physically incompetent and eventually causes panic. From what we understand Mr. Lincoln, you can tell us more about that than we can."

He gave a sheepish grin. "Yes, it scared the hell out of me. I would have given anything to get out of the workshop. Did you leave it running over lunch to booby trap me or what?"

Mark intervened.

"No Eddy – were sorry about that, it was a soak test for the circuit, to make sure all the design criteria were right and it wouldn't fail. You were not meant to be in here until later if you remember."

He nodded in agreement – it was his own fault.

"Is that it then – just this little board?"

David the biker stepped forward. Pointing to the test racks and around the workshop where there were ten or twelve small speaker units he said, "No, the signal generator feeds those two three hundred watt amplifiers over there and they in turn drive all those tweeters, the high frequency speakers. The push out about 150 decibels, which at lower frequencies, would destroy both your eardrums and cochlea and deafen you. At this frequency however it is inaudible to most people. Some will sense a kind of presence, and detect the edge of a sound, but they won't be able to tie it down. Nevertheless, for all those exposed to it, it will have a profound effect."

It was a remarkable demonstration and he said so.

"So this system we set up in the shop spliced in to the anti-intruder network. It fires up if anyone breaks in and makes them very, very reluctant to stay."

Mark nodded but raised a hand to censor further supposition.

"Yeah, it's okay up to a point Eddy but won't do a thing if the sound levels around it are very high and blanket the output from this. Competing sound swamps the effect – it's good in a comparatively silent environment but not otherwise. It would be useful against a single intruder stealing stuff in a silent environment, but would be unlikely to stop those taking part in a ram raid attack – too much noise you see, not only from the break in but engine noise and their vandalising the stock they want out of the way."

He stood back, disappointed a little but at least encouraged by the first part of Mark's comments.

"Well boys, better than nothing – it's a better safety net than the one we have at present."

David spoke up once again.

"It's not the sum total of what we can do Mr. Lincoln – this is only the beginning. We've done some digging and we know that acoustic weapons have been the subject of military research since the early 1950's – the French developed a very low frequency, that is an infrasound weapon, working at 7 cycle per second in 1954. It failed because it was only a short-range device and it wouldn't work effectively as a battlefield weapon. But it caused enormous physiological damage to animals under test close up. Now, we here aren't working on a battlefield weapon – we just want to dissuade ram raiders from completing what they expect to do. Dimensionally our shop isn't anything like a battlefield - so we think a low frequency system could work."

Mark and Robert nodded their agreement and waited for his confirmation to proceed.

It was Hobson's choice– what else did they have to protect their business and livelihood?

"Seems to me that we need to saturate the whole area with these vibrations. That would need a special set up wouldn't it?"

"No!" Mark said, "We would simply wire up every low frequency loudspeaker in the place so that they would all operate simultaneously. Let's face it, with all the huge power available from the guitar speakers, all the Hi-fi cabinets and everything else on the shelves, and adding all the tweeters at a very low cost, a combined system would not in any way look out of place. Yet its very normality would hide a very nasty surprise for intruders. All we would have to do, for the interim at least, is sacrifice two or possibly three of the *Elite 1000* one kilowatt public address amplifiers to drive the combined system. After that we link it into the burglar anti intruder alarm and let it sit there. It has no detrimental effect on the business, it will be easy to switch out any one set of speakers for a customer to listen to."

He stood mesmerised by Marks revelation - it sounded so very neat and straightforward. What reason was there not to allow them to go ahead? He looked down again at the tiny circuit board they had tested on him. He pitied any one stupid enough to attempt more than two minutes in the shop with that thing operating. God alone knew what they would experience under the proposal from Mark and his two assistants. Whatever it was, he hoped he would not be there when they did.

"Okay - do it. However, let me know if you are about to test the second system, I would prefer to be elsewhere."

They all smiled and acknowledged gratefully. It was going to be an interesting project.

He was just about to invite Mark into his office for another discussion on business expansion when Janice knocked on the workshop door and came into the workshop.

"Mr. Lincoln, there are two sign fitters outside in the shop, they say they are here to fit a new sign to the front of the shop. Is it okay?"

He turned to Janice. "Yes, tell them to go ahead, but before you do, please tell Mr. Stapleford that he should supervise the fitting."

He looked round at Mark who had a combined look of puzzlement and astonishment etched on his face.

"Why me Eddy – and why a new sign?"

He laughed – Mark was in for one hell of a surprise.

13

Time had slipped by and much of the shop's activities had settled into a regular, everyday pattern – not that anyone got bored. He watched with pleasure the subtle bonding of his staff, and the way they could stand either as individuals or as an integrated team. Their willingness to help, remove a difficulty or solve a problem, even though it might not be directly their responsibility, gave him and Mark some reassurance that their way of managing the business had its merits.

It was getting towards Christmas and Mark was with him in his office discussing the size of the staff Christmas bonus.

"You don't want to know the size of your bonus do you Mark?"

They both laughed. Mark knew very well that the recent signing of the partnership papers had in effect made him financially very well off. It was clear that his gratitude towards his erstwhile boss was boundless, but the idea of a bonus had nothing like the effect a few weeks back of seeing the new *Lincoln & Stapleford* shop sign go up and of hearing the applause from everyone in the shop as it was fixed into position; even a few customers had joined in.

"Let's make it a two weeks salary for the boys, the girls can have four weeks wages – okay?"

Mark nodded his head in agreement.

"Seems fair – though the sale people are due for a bonus at the end of the month – they'll win if everybody else is on an even playing field. Sam Hill's sales bonus is going to be substantial

– one for well over twenty thousand pounds on a single system. One other thing, though it's not strictly relevant, Sam has been successful in getting a Criminal Injuries Compensation payout. How's that for irony. Thought you might see the paradox in that."

"Christ – that means that they accept he was the victim and not the perpetrator. Jesus – what a contradictory and absurd mess."

He shook his head in bewilderment.

"Okay, nothing we can, or need to do there, Sam's entitled to the money. Now, back to bonuses, I revise my offer." You're right – Sam and Peter will always be ahead but that's what sales are about. Without their sales record the shop can't survive."

Mark looked uncomfortable for a moment.

"True – but the workshop does its bit – twelve per cent of the takings remember. I'd feel happier if my two were better rewarded. Remember, they did a hell of a lot of work designing and testing the anti-intruder systems. Come on Eddy! Think of all the insurance premiums we're saving."

That did indeed make him think.

He had no need to be reminded of the three week-ends Mark and the boys had given up to wire the two acoustic systems into the shop. Nor the fact that David had contrived the use of an old farm building to test it – apparently disabling three chickens, a sheep and a goat to prove it worked.

"Okay – your chaps get three weeks above salary as a thank you, Sam and Peter get two weeks above salary and their bonuses, and the girls three weeks too.

Mark grinned, "Always knew you were a pushover Eddy – but I'm sure everyone will appreciate the generosity. Anyway, the Christmas sales are coming on well and our takings will swamp the bonuses we give to the staff."

He agreed, thankful that the thorny problem of who gets what was resolved.

"All right Mark, now to other things. I take it you are still in support of expansion, especially as regards selling our own branded equipment. If so, I would like you to start pressing ahead with it. We need R&D costs, production and distribution figures and whether we can sell enough without having to distribute to other outlets. If the latter is necessary we need strong intellectual property protection.

Mark sat back, a tight, impassive smile on his face.

"Well, I've already dug out some of my designs and had the boys look at them for any glaring deficiencies. So far so good, but finding a manufacturer with the capacity to do what we want, particularly with the expertise needed, is problematic. I've only identified two possible partners and both want a substantial up-front payment to do all the pre- production engineering and manufacturing cost analysis to establish if the project is viable."

"How much is substantial Mark?"

"In both cases about £12,000. It's too much!"

It was a lot of money, but he already knew he was going to agree it – hell, what was £12,000 compared to what Mark had done for him in the past.

"Choose the one that you have the most confidence in and agree the payment – I have a feeling it will be worth it."

Marks face beamed with delight.

"Okay Eddy – thanks."

As he spoke there was a knock on the door.

"Come in." he called out.

Sam Hill entered, the scar on his face now faded to an almost indistinguishable line separating his normal skin.

"Hello Sam – what's new?"

"Peter's got a bee in his bonnet about a big black SUV that has passed the shop four times in the last half hour. It's not the passing that's got him worried – it's the fact that they are taking photographs of the shop as they pass. He thought you should know."

Mark and he locked eyes – Mark showing a degree of concern, as no doubt he did. "Press maybe – doing a follow up after the court case?"

He thought otherwise, though Mark had every reason to say what he did.

"What to do Mark? You could be right but better safe than sorry. Report it to the police?"

Mark scowled. "Might as well – they're bloody useless but you never know."

Mark turned and addressed Sam.

Sam, did you or Peter get the registration number?"

"Peter got it."

"Okay Sam, tell Peter to report it to the police and make sure we take the usual close-down precautions tonight. Clear?"

Sam withdrew with a wave of his hand acknowledging the instructions.

"Could be trouble Mark – can we rely on our deterrents?"

Mark raised an eyebrow. "More than we can the police – I'd bet money on it."

Nothing else marred the run up to the Christmas break and everything appeared to be promising a bumper sales figure. The girls in the office spent an inordinate amount of time decorating the shop but it paid dividends. Customer throughput peaked and there were times when Peter and Sam had to call on him to help out in the shop. Even the music section received an inordinate number of what seemed to be cash-rich patrons. The stock room started to look bereft of supply and there was a distinct danger that display items in the shop itself would have to be sold. Mark was very reluctant to allow it to happen, not least because many products on display were wired in as part of the anti-intruder system.

By Christmas Eve it was clear that they would get by, and as the shutters went down at midday there was a sense of excitement and achievement in everyone.

He waved goodbye to all as they departed for a week's shutdown leaving only Mark as the one remaining member of the gang.

"I trust you and Fiona are going to enjoy yourselves Mark. I hear you have most of the family staying with you, so you won't lack company."

Mark looked slightly guilty.

"Well, it's one of the penalties or joys - depending on your disposition - for having a very disperse but close knit family. Add Fiona's to mine and we could fill the national stadium. You won't forget will you Eddy, you're invited for Christmas dinner."

It was something he would not forget, it being the only chance he would get to join any Christmas festivities.

"No way, Mark, I'm really looking forward to it. I'll be there."

He gave Mark's arm a slight touch to demonstrate his gratitude. Mark in turn held out his hand.

"Eddy, I find it hard to thank you for all you have done. I doubt I could have found a more decent and empathetic person to call a colleague and friend."

As he shook Mark's hand he thought of all the reasons he could so easily reciprocate the tribute his partner had paid him.

"No Mark, how could I ever adequately repay the person that

saved my life? Now it's time for you to see your family – I'll see you all on the 25th."

Mark smiled and released his hand.

"Bear with me Eddy – I'm just going to do a final check on the detection systems and the deterrents. I hate going home in the car and then suddenly being brought to a halt by the thought that they had not been activated."

He smiled; Mark could always be trusted to do the right thing.

As he buttoned his coat, looked for his gloves and checked he had his car and shop keys, Mark returned.

"Okay, video, noise and optical sensors are on and the deterrent systems are all active and functioning. Let's hope we don't need any of it. Fingers crossed eh?"

They gave a crossed finger sign to each other and made for the door. Then he stopped mid-stride.

"Mark, I take it the electronics for the deterrent system are well hidden – we should avoid making it obvious."

Mark smiled, "They are where they should be, mixed in with the electronics for the standard sensors and detectors. I made sure that it is virtually impossible to isolate one from the other. As for the amplifiers, they appear to be for repair and are wired in as part of a CD system that has an FM radio link. It will appear as a normal music system to other eyes but in our case can pick up the deterrent signals as well, depending on which frequency you choose. Every time we go home I simply switch the signal source from one to the other and hey presto!"

He should have guessed – to think Mark had failed to see a chink in the armour was so improbable that it was not worth considering.

He gave Mark a slap on the back and a farewell wave. "The 25th then – I look forward to it."

Mark had gone by the time he brought down the steel door shutter and had checked each of the ones protecting the windows. He gave the now heavily barricaded shop one last look and then noted the few shoppers walking the pavements, most still scurrying around desperate to get last minute Christmas presents.

As he made for the rear of the shops to look for his car, he suddenly felt a sense of loss. To be alone at Christmas needed a high degree of resilience and self-reliance; they were the things that precluded loneliness when one was confined to a big house with lots of heartbreaking reminders and memories. In terms of resilience and self-reliance, he just hoped he had enough.

14

He spent most of the evening amusing himself by watching some of the top-flight movies broadcast for the holiday period. His evening meal was for once bought in. He managed to get lucky (so he thought) by getting the local curry shop to deliver a full chicken madras on a Christmas Eve. He was surprised when the delivery driver – obviously one of the shop's family – arrived at six p.m. and told him that he would be on duty for at least another seven hours. Christmas Eve, he said, was a busy time for the curry shop and they made hay while the sun shone.

The meal was particularly delicious and his spirits rose accordingly as his full stomach telegraphed contentment and satisfaction. His timing was good too, as the last plate went into the dishwasher the TV announced the start of a film he was looking forward to seeing. With that, he turned off the kitchen TV monitor, walked to the lounge and collapsed into his favourite armchair in front of the main TV screen. For all his past sorrows, he was anticipating a good Christmas day with Mark and his family, a gathering he hoped that would be devoid of any ghosts or reasons to be cheerless. He deserved no less.

Christmas morning found him late in leaving his bed. The bright sky reflected down on a sharp hoar frost but he discounted the weather; it had little chance of marring the day. By 11.00 a.m.

he was dressed and ready for departure – he felt a slight thrill of excitement, it was a feeling long forgotten but welcome just the same.

Mark's house was crowded with innumerable adults and children, none of whom seemed to stay in any one room or place for more than a minute. Mark had opened the door to him and immediately apologized for the chaos.

"Come and get a drink Eddy; as and when possible I'll introduce you to all and sundry."

But it didn't happen – not immediately. Mark and he found a vacant space in the conservatory and tried to have a conversation, but the background noise of a TV, over excited and squabbling children, adults trying to organise matters in the kitchen while attempting to discipline the kids, not to mention the gaggle of mothers and grandmothers in the lounge periodically bursting out into hysterical laughter, made the chat between them virtually impossible. Instead they simply kept refilling their glasses with sherry and vodka so that by the time Fiona came round calling everyone into the dining room for dinner, they were both feeling very well lubricated.

As he and Mark walked into what was a very large dining room the rest of the party, all eighteen, were already seated at the table and were trying on paper party hats.

Mark stopped and without hesitation shouted out. "Please be quite everyone."

Except for one child who did eventually lapse into silence, everyone stopped talking immediately and looked towards the speaker.

"My friends and loved ones – I haven't been able to introduce my friend and partner Edmund Lincoln until now – you have all been too busy or preoccupied – but I want to tell you how proud and pleased I am to be able to introduce you to him now. I don't have to tell you how generous and supportive he was during our encounter with the law and some of you will have met him during the trials. I can honestly say that had it not been for Edmund, we would not now be enjoying this Christmas day or our Christmas dinner. I would like everyone to show their appreciation by honouring Edmund with a round of applause."

He stood gratified and somewhat embarrassed by the thunderous response the guests gave him. It suddenly seemed that all that he had done over the past ten months had been worth it. His self-esteem and sense of worth was boosted to unparalleled heights by the reception he was receiving.

Mark slipped slightly behind him as the clapping started to subside and he felt him come closer. Mark leaned forward as he absorbed the pleasure of the applause and spoke into his ear.

"Edmund, Fiona and I want you to know that we will forever be in your debt and will never forget what you did for everyone. Fiona's too shy to say it but she wanted you to be particularly welcome. Your place at table is at the head – you are the guest of honour. We hope the small package you see there at your place will please you. Merry Christmas."

As he turned to thank Mark, Fiona and another woman came in each of them carrying a huge silver plate – one with a full roast chicken, the other a turkey.

He smiled at Fiona, slightly at a loss now that the applause had died down.

She returned the smile, "Come on Eddy – guest of honour carves!"

It was an uproarious and delightful dinner. Fiona and her kitchen helpers had spread the menu as far, and as tastefully, as it could go, and as he swallowed the last mouthful of Christmas pudding and fresh cream he realised, even with a sustained pang of loss for his darling Carol, it was perhaps the best Christmas he could remember.

The whole table, children and all, had reached a state of complete joy and elation, culminating in most of the intoxicated adults seeing hilarity in every silly antic arising. He was almost the last to leave the table, due to Fiona insisting he have 'just a little bit more'. He complied, had one more mouthful and, utterly bloated, finally reached his limit.

Completely satiated he staggered out of the dinning room into the lounge and found himself warmly content and rather tipsy after sinking into a fireside armchair. On his wrist, heavy and unfamiliar, was the Stapleford's present, a brand new solid gold Omega wrist watch - something he would never normally have bought for himself, but truly welcome nevertheless.

He surfaced just after six p.m. and realised he was feeling for the first time in a very long time, a sense of peace and contentment. The day had rejuvenated his optimism and his contentment with life.

Had he known that fate was to play a cruel and malicious trick on him he may well have thought otherwise. As it was, and unbeknown to him, he had four days of respite before the halcyon days were over.

15

He slept in on the 29th, promising himself as he awoke, a large brunch and then a trip out to explore the outside world and stretch his legs. It was dawning on him that he was too focused on the shop and business, and he was inheriting a very small world shackled by routine and habit. It was becoming somewhat stifling, and he decided that he needed to expand his horizons or risk turning into a sad, single minded and lonely hermit. There was no reason not to enjoy the benefits of a successful business as long as he avoided extravagance and self-indulgence.

So, he enjoyed a leisurely brunch and left the house just after 11.30 a.m. He nosed the car out of the driveway expecting to see the usual traffic jam that occurred on the stretch of road on which he lived. Today he was presented with two virtually empty lanes, reminding him thankfully that the Christmas break was far from over.

He gunned the car left onto the nearest lane and settled down to drive. Where he was going he had no idea, but that was the whole purpose of a random exploration. Wherever the road went he would go. He remembered with some amusement the old maxim *'you should never worry about where you are going because no matter where you go, there you are!'*

He was three miles down the road when to his annoyance his mobile phone rang.

He pulled in to a bus stop lay-by, hoping that the holiday

schedule would reduce the chances of him being forced out by an irate bus driver. However, there was no one standing at the bus stop so he was on to a reasonable bet in his favour.

He pressed the receive button and heard Mark's voice.

"Eddy, are you there?"

"Yeah, hello Mark, to what do I owe the pleasure, in short, given the tone of your voice, what's the trouble?"

"Bad news Eddy. I can't believe I'm saying this – I've just heard that the shop has been hit. The bastards went in through the rear security door – thermic lance apparently. But that's not the all of it – they're dead – all five who broke in are dead. We need to get there Eddy – quickly. Can you pick me up please? Fiona's got the car – she's gone off on a jolly with some of her family and with the rest of the tribe also absent I've no transport."

As Mark spoke, his words came like a solid bolt of spiritual destruction. Something paralysed his breathing and he almost fainted as each disclosure sunk in. His hand started to shake, making the mobile vibrate against his ear.

He could only whisper back.

"Yes, hang on Mark, I'm already on the road, I'll be with you in... about... twenty minutes."

Mark was standing outside the house as he drove up. He came to a halt just long enough for Mark to drag open the door and throw himself into the passenger seat. The car was already moving at a pace as Mark tried to fit his seat belt and as the buckle locked into place he looked to his right.

"Never bloody rains but it pours Eddy, God only knows how all this came about."

"How did you find out Mark – police?"

"Yeah – you weren't contactable on your land line number – they phoned me instead."

"That's a bloody miracle – I would have laid bets that they were all down at the local pub celebrating their complete an utter incompetence."

Mark held on to a grim face.

"Well, somehow they discovered the break in and apparently found five bodies inside the shop. I hate to say it, but we had best keep quite about our anti-intruder system. I have a bad feeling that the system is responsible for the present circumstances."

He looked round at Mark, seeing only his side view but for all that noting that Mark was unable to disguise a bleak and tense expression.

As the high street came in view the shop front clearly stood out but there was no sign of any damage to the two steel shutters protecting the display windows. A lone policeman patrolled the outside pavement – kicking his heels and looking intensely bored. As they approached, the policemen motioned with his right hand, indicating the rear access road that served the whole line of shops for deliveries.

He turned the car left and after twenty yards quickly right which revealed the whole of the service road. As they stared through the car windscreen it was clear the authorities were in attendance. Three police cars, two ambulances and two unmarked private cars were parked alongside the high wall that bordered the outer side of the service road. Further down was another vehicle, a black SUV with the rear lid open.

He brought the car to a stop – twenty yards from the crime scene tape that stretched across the service road.

"Mark, that black wagon over there – care to bet that it's the one Sam and Peter eyeballed last week?"

Mark nodded.

"Yeah, I'm also willing to bet that they reconnoitred the front and the back of the shop to find the weakest point. Never would have guessed that they'd take out the rear door, it was once the strongest point in our security."

He shook his head in disgust. "I guess you don't account for things like a thermic lance – who the hell would have thought it? Let's see how bad it is."

He nosed the car further forward and stopped just before the tape.

As they exited the car he looked at the rear entrance of the shop. The metal security door was lying to one side of the entrance, each hinge a blackened and distorted parody of its original shape. Now the hinges were no more than frozen blobs of what had once been boiling, dripping metal. Likewise the lock, where it had been was now replaced by a large misshapen hole surrounded by the cooled residue of molten steel.

He looked around, noting that for all the vehicles in view there was not a single policeman or any other individual in sight. It did not faze him: the complete lack of activity was not surprising.

As he and Mark ducked under the security tape, two paramedics appeared pushing out a stretcher through the half closed ambulance doors. The empty body bag on the stretcher gave credence to what Mark had heard from the police.

As they made their way forward two other men exited the security door and halted as he and Mark came forward.

One carried a bag, the other, taller, was dressed in casual clothes and appeared to be a civilian.

"Who are you –what are you doing here?" The taller man challenged.

They stopped.

"My name is Edmund Lincoln, this gentleman is Mark Stapleford, if you care to look at the sign over the front of the shop you will see that we are the principal partners here. Now, who the hell are you?"

The smaller man carrying the bag obviously had no interest in the exchange, whatever its outcome. He looked up at his taller companion.

"I'll press on Chief Inspector, once I've had these bodies on the slab I hope to be able to give you a more accurate report. Good day."

The bag and the smaller man hurried off, leaving him and Mark glaring at the policeman.

The detective's face gave no hint of being conciliatory.

"Yes of course," came a monotonic reply, "you were called earlier. From what I understand from sources, this isn't your first episode of being raided. I'm familiar with your well-publicised court case earlier this year, but as I remember that event was not instigated by a full-scale burglary. This, I'm afraid, is not only a major criminal strike but a virtually unique one. As you may have been told, not one of those involved appeared to have survived the break in. They are all dead. May I ask..."

As he was talking he was moved aside by two more paramedics who were manoeuvring three folded stretchers back into the shop.

The policemen turned to the two men going in.

"Be careful, some of the partition wall is dangerously cracked and the fifth body is under the section where the ceiling collapsed. You'll see the legs."

He turned back.

Where was I ... oh yes, I'm going to escort you into your premises gentlemen; we have to await a full forensic team to investigate this crime scene. Being Christmas, it's slowing things down somewhat, so I can't let you have free access for the moment. Oh, and since you ask, my name is Saxby, Detective Chief Inspector Saxby. Follow me please."

16

The corridor leading towards the shop passed the stock room and the admin office, but here there appeared to be no sign of damage or disturbance. However, as they reached the screening door between the corridor and the shop display area they had every reason to be dismayed. Only weak, ghostly light from three still functioning strip lights illuminated the rear of the shop. The feeble winter daylight coming in through the display windows only added enough illumination for the front part of the floorspace; in combination the overall poor lighting created a shadowy perspective of sagging ceiling panels, cracked tiles, broken brickwork and powdered mortar from the partly demolished dividing wall separating the two display areas. To one side a whole line of shelves listed forward or hung by a single remaining bracket. On the floor all around lay piles of overturned and broken speakers, dust covered amplifiers and a complete shelf of CD units all having fallen in such a way as to appear to have been piled one on top of the other.

As he looked, his eyes fell on the paramedics who were zipping up a body that had fallen in the middle of the audio sales floor. Close to was another, this one on his back with a contorted, open-mouthed face, made the more horrific by a dusting of chalk white powder which surrounded the now dark pits of wide open eyes, once screwed up to counter excruciating pain. Like his face his dark clothes were covered in a chalk white residue evidently overlaid on him after he had died and stopped moving. To the extreme right, where some of the ceiling had broken loose, a pair of legs protruded out of the heap of tiles and metal framework that had come down. These legs too had taken on the look of a snowman, only the orange soles of a pair of trainers contrasted with the powder white.

He followed Mark, who moved through the debris like a semi-paralysed automaton, saying nothing but doggedly following the steps of Saxby as the policeman took the lead in exploring the interior more fully. In truth there was little to be said as the full horror of the scene began to register.

He stayed behind the other two – surveying as best he could what the true extent of the damage actually was.

It was as though they had been the victims of a half-hearted raid. Yes, there was damage, but even with the poor lighting it was obvious it was not going to take much to rectify it. Certainly it was nothing like as bad as the previous extremely destructive ram raid. The only thing that made him wary of being optimistic was the evidence of five dead burglars, and he had a very good idea of how, and why, they died.

Saxby had turned to face them; his whole body in shadow as the weak light backlit him. The thin, gaunt face was now virtually indistinct, and although he was speaking it wasn't possible to see his lips move. Only the odd emphatic movement of his head gave any life to his words.

"Earlier, as you gentlemen arrived, I intended to ask you if you had any idea of how this situation could have occurred. In all the years I have been an investigating officer I have never known a break in like this to cause the death of a burglar. Dead burglars yes, but invariably due to their own negligence or recklessness. This is different. Every one of these men died from unknown causes and the pathologist who you saw earlier is for the moment baffled. Can you two gentlemen shine a light on this – can you think of anything here that could have caused their deaths?" Without hesitation, he and Mark answered "No!"

17

They said very little to one another on the way back, it was only when Mark realised they were not navigating along the route back to his own house that he objected.

"It's okay Mark, I need an hour of your time so please stick with me. I've had to think of a few things since we left the shop – you need to know what it is."

What he had decided was, as far as he could see, the only course of action open to him, and although he knew Mark would protest vehemently there was little alternative.

As he pulled the car into the driveway he had much of what he had intended to say to Mark already composed in his head – he just hoped that ultimately his friend would see the sense of it.

He got out of the car and immediately made for the front door choosing not to speak a word for the interim – he needed to create a slight distraction and since he was dry and shaken by the experience at the shop, a strong coffee was in order.

"Mark, grab a seat in the lounge – I'm making coffee."

As the kettle boiled he thought back to what Saxby had said as they left the shop to travel back. They would not be able to take possession of the shop for at least a few days, not until all the forensic examinations were completed, and he would be grateful, so he said, if they would both report to the local police station as soon as possible to make a statement.

He also remembered Saxby's reaction when he and Mark had

emphatically denied knowing the cause of the burglars deaths – for what seemed an interminable ten seconds, Saxby's tall figure had remained a black unmoving silhouette in the semi- darkness of the shop. When at last he responded it was a simple, but knowing, "Okay."

He found Mark sitting in the lounge staring fixedly at the blank screen of the TV. As he proffered Mark's mug of coffee it was plain that Mark was deep in thought, reflecting on the morning's events and trying to find a way of extricating all involved from a potentially dangerous situation.

"Mark...hey Mark – your coffee!"

Mark gave a slight twitch of his head, and as he surfaced from his thoughts he reached out for the mug.

"This is bloody awful Eddy – you know the trouble we are in? Christ, we had no idea the sound field would be lethal. We tested it in some farm buildings on animals and it gave no indication that a human could be harmed by it. The whole idea was to make the shop space an unbearable environment and drive the crooks away – not kill them! O, Lord what a mess!"

He sat opposite Mark, watching his anxiety escalate. It wasn't unexpected; Mark had more to lose than he did.

"Listen Mark, I've thought about this too. What's happened has happened – it's no good bemoaning the fact. We need to work out what we intend to do in the event the same thing happens as it did the last time... after the incident with that maniac Dighton I mean. I will tell you now that I won't have you and your family implicated – if a prosecution follows on from all this, I will accept the consequences."

Mark looked as though he had taken a physical blow.

"Oh, come on Eddy - you can't mean that. Think of all..."

"I have Mark. Look around you – see any kids, Carol? Where is my family – absent without leave I'm sad to say. So you see, I have a lot less to lose than you or anyone else in the firm. In any case, if I can absolve you from a prosecution you can at least hold things together. If we both get nailed everything goes to the dogs – you, the staff, the business and me. Remember, I okayed the deterrent system, I was as eager to solve the insurance problem as anyone. I'm as much to blame as if I had wired up the electronics myself, so don't start quibbling about who should take responsibility."

Mark stared, wide-eyed and aghast.

"Christ Eddy, surely you can't be serious, if this all goes bad you could be facing a long time behind bars."

"I know, I'm ready to take the consequences, but that doesn't mean I'm going to capitulate from the start. If the police do decide to bring charges they are going to have a hell of a hard time of it."

Mark took a sip from his coffee. "How – how do we make it hard for them?"

"Well first we ignore Saxby – we don't go near the police station and we certainly won't make statements. Let them formulate a case without any help from us. Next I'm going to see Nathan Elliot so that this time we have an expert legal brain on our side. Then, if things do go pear shaped we will ensure the press are well briefed. We fucked up the CPS once before because of public pressure – we can do it again. My gut feeling is that if the whole story gets aired in court, no jury will convict me. Just like before."

Mark shrugged. "Hell of a risk though Eddy – you never know."

"Yes I do – I told you, whatever happens I'm prepared for it, good or bad."

"So, what else do we do in the meantime other than keeping our fingers crossed?"

He smiled – what use a business if it can't operate?

"That's easy Mark, as soon as we get possession of the shop again we'll start putting things back together. Can't let those bastards who broke in damage the livelihoods of our people can we? The damage isn't catastrophic – it shouldn't take too long. I want us up and running again as soon as possible. Now, how about another coffee?"

18

For a while he was on tenterhooks waiting for the axe to fall. Even as he and Mark busied themselves with getting the shop refurbished and refitted, and trying to solve the problems of staff and customers having to work around the tradesmen as they repaired everything, he was constantly thinking of the day he would be arrested.

DCI Saxby had made just the one visit to ask why he and Mark had failed to make statements. They had simply stated that they had nothing to hide or say but in any case, their legal advice was to say nothing. When Saxby had pointed out that having nothing to hide would be revealed in any statement they made, they both laughed.

They were fully aware of the traps the law provided for unwary innocents, they told him, and they had no intention of falling into one.

Then they asked Saxby why the police were so serious about establishing the circumstances and cause of death of the raiders. After all, it appeared from what the papers were saying that the police were satisfied that the same team had been responsible for several raids up and down the country and had constantly escaped the police by fleeing back to Europe after every break in. Their demise eliminated the need for a large but failed police investigation and the subsequent embarrassment. As such, what was Saxby's motive, some kind of vendetta driven by misguided principles?

Saxby had taken the comment with a sour face but was in no position to do more. He vacated the shop after a cursory look at the repair work being carried out – though he took more interest in the amplifiers and speakers still on display. As he made for the exit he stopped and bent his head behind some of the monitor speakers. He inspected the wiring as though searching for an answer, but his whole demeanour gave the impression of someone impotent and at a loss to understand an enigma. He and Mark watched with some disquiet – Saxby clearly had suspicions.

With Saxby gone Mark went back to look at the cabinet containing the anti-intruder and deterrent circuitry. He came back to report that he had no reason for concern - whatever the forensic teams, or anyone else, had done there was no sign of tampering or interference, it was all still intact.

By the third week after the break in the media reports had died down and most of the refurbishment work had been completed. At first the reporters and cameramen had been frustrated by the refusal of the two partners and any of the staff to give interviews. Mark had expressly forbade Robert and David in the workshop to say anything to anyone regarding the acoustic deterrent, assuring them that they would not be implicated regardless of the outcome of any inquiries. Since no one else had any real understanding of what had transpired or why, the rest of the staff were told that it would be in their long-term interests to avoid the press and anyone else trying to pries information out of them.

For a while there had been a tense atmosphere around the shop and even the customers seemed to be staying away, but only a month passed before everything, including sales, appeared to be returning to normal. Even the harsh February and early March weather had only a temporary effect on turnover; most of the lost internal shop sales being compensated for by Internet and telephone orders.

There came a time when he and Mark began to think that they had escaped any indictment. But then a date was announced for a coroner's inquest into the deaths of the five burglars and the press reopened the whole fiasco. The outcome of the coroner's hearing was crucial so Elliot told them, for it explored whether or not the deaths of the five men had been a lawful or unlawful killing, or whether the cause could not be established. In the latter case it would result in an open verdict.

It was a bitterly cold mid March morning when they parked the car and shivered their way from the car to the coroner's court. Because the case had been well publicised, and had taken front page reports in some of the national papers, the court was mainly populated by chilled and disgruntled press reporters, all wishing they were still in bed. He took a forward seat with Mark being two of perhaps a handful of curious attendees not involved with the press. Some were probably there just to temporally escape the cold and thankful that the court itself was reasonably warm. The court doors were only opened for those wishing to enter, being kept shut otherwise by a pair of pragmatic officials intent on keeping the freezing wind out and themselves warm.

It was not long before a clerk called out "All stand for Her Majesty's coroner." A chilled throng of heavily clothed and pinch faced observers dragged themselves to their feet and stood reluctantly as the coroner hurried in.

The coroner, a ruddy faced and portly local solicitor, his robes hiding thickly padded clothes, called for order.

The terms of the inquiry were read; that the inquiry was intended to establish the cause of death of five men, all of unknown nationality or identity, taking part in a robbery and found dead at the scene of the crime. There being no identification, and thus no relatives or immediate public disquiet, no jury would be called. The reason the inquiry had been opened was that the deaths were unusual and apparently unnatural, and it was in the public interest to examine the circumstances under which they died.

He sat with a somewhat fidgety Mark who was more anxious than he was. It was probable that Mark was not aware that the coroner's court had a very limited brief, to establish cause of death but not to expose or indict anyone for its occurrence. He leaned over and whispered, "This court has no power to arrest or accuse. Calm down."

Mark looked solemn but nodded.

The first witness was the pathologist called to the shop after the discovery of the five dead men.

The coroner waited for the pathologist to appear in the witness box, to identify himself, and then gather his notes. The pathologist did so with an air of reluctance; wearing a thick overcoat and a scarf, he gave the impression that it was far too cold to take part in the proceedings and he would have preferred to have given his evidence from his bed.

"Dr. Murray, what are your findings as regards the five deceased?"

The pathologist coughed and scanned his notes again.

"There is a degree of controversy regarding this sir. I have consulted the three most expert pathologists in the country in this matter and taken the best possible advice.

All of the men found dead in the circumstances described were

116

aged between twenty-five and thirty-five. They were all, save one, in reasonably good health. On initial examination none of the men had suspicious external injuries, certainly nothing life threatening that took place pre or post mortem other than slight bruising and some abrasions found on one man who was found under a collapsed ceiling. These injuries I hasten to add were not the cause of his death. In every case, except one, the cause of death was massive internal disruption of vital organs leading to severe haemorrhaging and subsequent abrupt lowering of blood pressure. This would invariably result in a slow loss of consciousness. This in turn would be followed fairly rapidly by what I can only describe as an unpleasant, if not agonising, death. The fifth man, found as I recall near the shop entrance, also exhibited internal damage but he died not from internal bleeding but from a coronary thrombosis. Given the man's degree of advanced heart disease, this could have happened at any time, but I can only conclude that what killed the other four men was also instrumental in hastening his death."

The coroner interrupted with an exasperated wave of his hand.

"Am I to understand that as yet you, and those you have consulted, are still unsure of the forces that created the physical conditions you describe? That what caused the internal damage to these men is still a mystery?"

The pathologist gave a perfunctory shake of his head.

"No − not completely. At first the collective evidence was very mystifying, four men had comparable internal disruption but there was apparently no precedence, nothing anyone knew of that could have caused it. However, one of the pathologists I consulted remembered a paper published in 1947 after Hiroshima and Nagasaki, in which a number of victims were found to have internal organ disruption. The huge shock wave experienced by the victims caused similar pathologies to the ones found on the four men in question. Likewise, earthquake victims and soldiers killed near explosive detonations – they too can exhibit internal disruption due to shock waves. At this time, one can only conclude that the deceased experienced something similar, yet how and why remains to my mind completely inexplicable."

The coroner paused for a moment apparently digesting the last comments from the pathologist. Though the court had warmed up somewhat, he and Mark felt a coldness heading their way.

"Dr Murray, is there anything relevant or incidental you can add to your testimony?"

Murray appeared to give a slight shrug.

"No sir, other than two discrepancies, or if you will, lack of common features in the deaths of the five men. Two of the men had ruptured eardrums; that is two of those found inside the shop. The one man found at the entrance, the man who suffered the cardiac arrest, did not. Two of the men inside the shop had what appeared to be scorch marks on their sleeves and wrists, none of the others did. I propose that this was not relevant to their deaths, that the thermic lance they used to break through the metal security door or during cutting inside the shop was responsible for the scorch marks."

The coroner nodded and then asked, "What are your final thoughts in terms of this remarkable incident?"

"Well sir, I cannot speak authoritatively for the cause of the forensic results but having a vivid recollection of the inside of the shop I would say that some kind of explosion, creating a powerful shock wave, killed – or helped to kill – these five men. The damage to the ceiling, brickwork and everything around seems to point in that direction. As to the men's identity, I believe that is still a matter of investigation by the police."

The coroner sighed, "My thanks Dr. Murray – next witness."

He felt Mark attempting to get more comfortable on the hard wooden bench that populated the court public area. He took the view that the benches had obviously been installed to discourage people from attending long court sessions. Even he was beginning to feel a distinct ache in his buttocks. And yet for all the discomfort he was to some extent relieved – the pathologist was less than certain of the cause of death and in the absence of anything more damning it was a reasonable bet that the verdict would not be 'unlawful killing'.

The man who now stepped in to the witness box was tall and thin. His hair was receding and the outside cold had clearly imposed a detrimental effect on his face – both cheeks being pinched and raw, creating red blotches contrasting against a sickly grey-white skin.

The coroner invited him to identify himself.

"Thank you sir. I am Dr. Alan Norman, senior forensic scientist at county police laboratories."

He coroner smiled ingratiatingly, it was clear that the one was already known to the other.

"Please let us have your report Dr. Norman."

"Sir, my team has completed its examination of the premises where the five men died. Our first conclusion is that whatever created the – let us call it a shockwave – was not initiated by conventional explosives. We found absolutely no trace of typical combustion or detonation products, nor any residue, of any known explosive. Similarly, the damage to the premises was not impact damage – that is, there was no seat of an explosion and no debris flying away to impact on other surfaces. If anything, and here I agree with the previous witness, the damage was similar to that caused by an earth tremor or a real earthquake.

In short, it appeared as though the place was shaken to bits by some overwhelming force. What we do know for certain is that no seismic activity of any significance occurred over the time the premises were occupied by the victims. As such we were faced with a perplexing puzzle, a puzzle that at first seemed intractable. However, the perpetrators used a thermic lance and on inspection the accelerator tubes, the lance being made up of sacrificial metals like magnesium and aluminium fed by a very high pressure oxygen cylinder, was improperly set up. To avoid a long and tedious explanation, it seems likely that oxygen was leaking during the whole time the five men were in the premises. We believe they took their thermic lance and the oxygen cylinders into the shop with them and started to use it on the safe and cash registers. We are of the opinion that leaking oxygen, mixed with an improperly loaded lance, formed a metal plume, which created an explosive atmosphere. Now this would cause an almost instantaneous mid-air detonation, with a flame front moving through the whole room very rapidly. The effect would be like a uniform shock wave travelling outward and every man would be hit by it. The pressure wave would have had a disastrous effect on the human body, much like being squeezed by a five-ton weight.

Although we are not absolutely comfortable with this hypothesis – that is, whether it is scientifically unassailable – we feel that in terms of what evidence we have, it is the only rational explanation."

The coroner turned with an apologetic tilt to his head.

"Dr. Norman, can you give the court a more extensive description of this evidence – without too much of an opaque account?"

Norman shook his head, "Only that we traced metallic particles on the back of four of the victims and on the front of two of them. It would indicate what position each was in when a shock wave carried the combusting particles towards them. Just like a...just like a sound wave... moving though the air. Yes, just like that..."

Norman suddenly hesitated and immediately looked thoughtful. He reached inside his jacket pocket and withdrew a pen, using it to hastily scribble on his small sheaf of notes. As he did so the coroner looked up.

"Do you wish to enlarge on that Dr. Norman?"

Norman registered the question with a vigorous shake of his head.

The coroner faced the court observing the expectant faces of those watching. He then took a moment to write into a small ledger in front of him after which he again addressed the court.

"In the absence of any further evidence or witnesses from the authorities, and as I understand it there are no family members of the deceased present this morning to shed further light on this matter, I can only come to one conclusion, that the five deceased, in pursuance of a criminal act, were killed by virtue of their own negligence. I am therefore obliged to declare a verdict of misadventure. This inquiry is closed."

As the court came to life with all those in the public seats now on their feet and happy to be released, he was suddenly caught with mixed feelings. On the one hand the verdict had not been 'unlawfully killed' which removed any indictment as far as he and Mark were concerned. Yet, the reaction of Dr. Norman when he had inadvertently used the idea of a 'sound wave' was ominous – there was no doubt he had developed a sudden and possibly enlightening idea. The fact that he had immediately made some notes after his disclosure implied he had something to pursue. It did not bode well.

19

In the car on return to the shop Mark stayed somewhat sullen and silent. It was only as they parked the car at the rear of the shop and espied the new security door that Mark broke his dark mood.

"I have a bad feeling about all this Eddy, I'm fairly certain that the guy from the forensics lab has got hold of an idea of what happened to the raiders. Regardless of the verdict this morning I think we can expect trouble."

As he removed his seat belt he had to admit that Mark was probably right. Dr. Norman was a scientist and armed with an extensive understanding of technology – if he thought that an ultra – powerful sound field had caused the deaths of the five men he would as likely want to verify it first and then investigate the shop for a similar set up.

As he exited the car Mark stood pensive and dejected, clearly at a loss to express his feelings.

"What's wrong Mark – you know we agreed what we would do if the shit hit the fan. Stop getting anxious over something that might not happen. Right now we simply disengage the deterrent system, lose it in a skip somewhere and pretend nothing ever happened. Okay?"

Mark looked up from his crestfallen stance.

"Yeah – right, but we lose all our protection... unless... unless we only disengage the low frequency side and leave the rest operational. I'm sure the low frequency sound radiation is the lethal element of the system so we'll dispense with it. You and I know just how effective the high frequency side is in making an intruder incompetent so we can be reasonably sure that in most circumstances it will still be a definite deterrent. All we need to do is switch out the low frequency signal generator - easy!"

It was clearly the sensible thing to do and he had no qualms about Mark's suggestion.

"Okay, let's do that. The moment we get in."

Mark stepped forward and walked to the new security door. He pulled hard at it, the new hinges still being stiff. As it came open they both entered the connecting corridor with Mark waiting behind him to re-close the door.

"Must get some oil on those hinges." Mark muttered to himself.

They passed the admin office door, the stock room and came up to the workshop entrance. The door was open and the workshop appeared to be empty, only the overhead lights and an oscilloscope displaying a signal trace indicated that the two assistant engineers had been at home earlier.

"Lunch." Mark said in explanation of the empty room.

"I'm going to do the necessary on the deterrent unit now - better no one watches me. I'll catch up with you in a moment."

He nodded his acknowledgement and continued towards the door leading to the shop and the display areas.

He pulled it open and stepped in to the rear of the shop.

Sam and Peter were behind the central counter looking at a small device and turned towards him as he entered.

"Morning - sorry, afternoon. Had your lunch yet?"

They grinned and shook their heads. "Not yet Mr. Lincoln, we were holding on until you and Mr. Stapleford returned. Anyway, we stagger our lunch breaks day on day. Sam first one day and me the next, I'm on the early lunch today." Peter Lansdale replied. He shook his head, "Not today boys, you can both go now, I'll take over for the next hour."

They grinned with appreciation and made for the corridor cloakroom – finding lunch in freezing conditions meant dressing like a Siberian nomad.

For the moment he left his topcoat on, ensuring he didn't cool to quickly after the car heater had brought them a momentary summer. As the two sales boys reappeared smothered in coats, scarves and gloves, he wished them a good lunch and watched them leave the shop heading up the high street to the fish and chip shop. He was fully aware of their tastes in food.

He gave all the displays and equipment a quick inspection, checked the cash register and order book and then decided to bring up some sound in the listening room. He had half turned to carry out his intention when he saw a police car draw up outside the shop. Almost in an instant three uniformed policemen and one in plain clothes emptied from the car and thrust their way through the entrance doors into the shop.

The plain-clothes man was well known to him – it was Saxby.

"Good afternoon Mr. Lincoln, I have a warrant to search these premises. Where is your partner Mr. Stapleford?"

He had steeled himself for this moment, but now that it had come he felt the first tremors of alarm. He braced himself for what could be his imminent arrest and held his dignity.

"A warrant Chief Inspector – may I see it."

Saxby dug into his topcoat inside pocket and withdrew a folded paper. He stepped forward and held it out.

He scanned the paper and read from it.

"It says 'in order to determine any instrument or device involved in the deaths of the following... Chief Inspector, surely you are aware that the coroner's verdict this morning was misadventure. I suspect that your enquiries are lagging behind both events and the law."

As he started to hand back the warrant to Saxby the connecting door to the corridor was pushed open and an unknown man walked into the shop. In his hands he held two electronic circuit boards.

"No one else in the place inspector, but we found these circuit boards next to the security system. It looks as if they were either being installed or removed. There's no way of knowing for sure."

It came as a shock – surely Mark had...!"

"Who are you?"

The unknown man had a deadpan face – he made the term inscrutable an overstatement.

"My names McPherson, I'm with Dr. Norman – county forensic team. I specialise in electronics. "

"Oh good – and what are you doing with those circuits?"

McPherson gave the hint of a smile and held up one of the boards.

"Well – the first thing is they are based on a standard audio signal generator chip, this one appears to be contrived for a very high frequency, and this one for a switchable set of low frequencies. On the same boards I see what appears to be a radio transmitter. That in itself is not directly of any significance...until I inspected three very powerful amplifiers in the workshop, two with the chassis open and the other on its back, making it appear as thought they were all under repair. Each had a radio receiver fitted into their circuitry meaning whatever these little boards in my hands were sending out, the amplifiers received and amplified. Connect these very powerful amplifiers to lots of speakers and I suspect the sound levels would be utterly overwhelming."

He saw Saxby smile – he didn't like it.

"Excuse me for saying so, but so what? They could simply be test boards made by the workshop people – they put together lots of circuits for specific tests, the circuit boards you have there could be perfectly innocent."

McPherson held up both boards in a dramatic show.

"Not these – I found them partially wired in to the security system – I took photographs to prove it. These were not used as testing boards; they were part of the anti-intruder system. Until I test the output of each board I can't be absolutely certain, but I'm of the opinion that the system was designed to be an intruder deterrent – a lethal one."

He turned to Saxby. "It's rubbish – shear speculation. I can think of a number of innocuous reasons why things are as they are. All you have to do is ask my partner and workshop manager, or any of his team – they'll clarify everything."

Saxby grinned, "I intend to, but in the meantime Mr. Lincoln you are under arrest on suspicion of unlawful killing pending further enquiries."

20

He found the police station custody cell claustrophobic and over-lit. The overhead fluorescents hanging from a highly reflective grey-white ceiling were harsh and oppressive and in no way diminished by the equally glossy dove-grey paint surrounding the whole cell. The high, steel barred window on the outer wall over- arched him, almost like a lancet shaped skylight. It was constructed from heavily painted but irregular and ugly brickwork and made his sense of confinement even worse.

The cell door was scratched with graffiti, irrespective of the big notice warning prisoners that it was an offence to damage or deface any part of the cell. It was still possible to see a slight brown trace where a previous inmate had painted 'Fuck you' in blood over the sign. To one side of the sign was a bell push, enabling him to call the duty constable responsible for prisoner's welfare.

When he had been booked in he had refused to co-operate in any way with the desk sergeant and on each question had replied with the standard 'No comment'.

Unfortunately the desk sergeant was his old friend sergeant Neilson who, with an obvious display of reluctance and regret, filled in the custody documents from memory.

With his shoelaces, belt and tie confiscated he was notified that a solicitor would be made available to him as soon as possible at his request. Instead of asking for an unknown duty solicitor to represent him, he asked for his own firm to make an appearance and hoped they would have the good sense to notify Nathan Elliot of his plight. As he paced the cell he kept his fingers crossed and went over the earlier proceedings in his mind.

First, how the hell had Mark managed to spirit himself away when the forensic man was searching the workshop? Second, how was it that Saxby and his cohort had arrived so soon after the coroner's verdict?

None of these queries had an immediate answer but he would find out in 24 hours if what he had been told about the limits of police custody were true. Only in serious cases could they ask for an extension if other enquiries were pending. Likewise, if his solicitors were slow in responding he might be cooped up for longer since he could not be interviewed without a solicitor being present. It was, as usual, a case of fingers crossed.

He was given some food at 6.00 p.m. and occasionally rang for a tea or coffee, but as the night came on he was finally thankful it was at last 'lights out'. He slept intermittently – not only because of his personal anxieties but because of the interruption from the noises coming from other occupied cells. At least one prisoner would periodically explode into frenzy. Erupting with cries of despair, the man would then go berserk for minutes at a time, screaming for release as he kicked and head butted his cell door. It made sleeping almost impossible.

When at last the dawn came he had made up his mind – what he had agreed with Mark he would adhere to absolutely and regardless – he was now convinced that if the prosecutors brought any charges against him he would fight them on his own. Indeed, the unexpected shock and bewilderment of being arrested when he was had now abated. His feeling was adamant; that he should never relinquish his unsympathetic attitude to the men who died in the shop during their break in. Not only that, he felt deeply aggrieved, as his team had with Dighton's case, that he should be facing criminal charges.

No, this time the stupid law would not go unchallenged or criticised. Of that he was completely and utterly determined.

They brought him breakfast at 7.00 a.m. - a fried sausage, a piece of bacon, fried bread and a tinned tomato. Badly cooked though it was, he wolfed it down as a reservoir against any ordeal to come.

He was released from the cell at 9.30 a.m. and led to an interview room. Though he entered by a different door, to his surprise it was the same room he had met Moran in after Dighton had been killed.

His solicitor, Simon Greenway was already there and greeted him as he came in.

"Good to see you Mr. Greenway, I trust you are aware of why I am here?"

Greenway was at least eight inches smaller than he was and his double-breasted suit seemed to wrap itself around him like a vertical brewers cask. However, rotund though he might be, his head contained a sharp brain and he had never failed to get things right.

"Hello Mr. Lincoln, yes I do now. I telephoned Mr. Elliot, he's in the middle of a case at the Old Bailey but it finishes today and he has promised to get down to see you as soon as possible. In the meantime we have to see what transpires. As I understand it, you are the only member of your team under arrest at the moment. Will Mr. Stapleford be making an appearance do you think?"

He gave Greenway a fixed look.

"I suspect not, in fact I hope not."

Greenway nodded and held out a hand to invite him to sit down. "I believe you are being held on suspicion of unlawful killing. As you know that can mean anything. They will have to come up with something more specific if you are to be brought before the magistrates for remand or release. It depends on...ah!"

The lower door to the interview room opened and DCI Saxby and another man came into the room. Saxby had a bundle of papers in his hand that flapped as he moved.

Saxby sat down opposite them and offered no greeting or comment. He laid the papers down and turned to the other man.

"Do the honours Compton."

They waited while the recorders on the shelf above them came to life and the identifications, dates and times were read out onto the recorders tape.

Saxby then scanned the top sheet of his bundle and after a few seconds looked across the table.

"The five men who died in your shop Mr. Lincoln died from ruptures of the internal organs caused by massively powerful vibrations emanating from within your shop. We know now how those vibrations were created – the forensic examination of the circuit boards and the amplifiers we found in you shop confirm that they were the source of a lethal trap for any intruder. The higher frequency board caused them to become so disorientated and confused that they were unable to escape the lower, more lethal, vibrations. Your system zapped them and then killed them. Am I right?"

"No comment."

"I have to tell you Mr. Lincoln that the evidence is undeniable – unless I get some cooperation from you I am inclined to interview everybody working for you and if necessary charge them with aiding and abetting. Do I make myself clear?"

Greenway interposed with a cough.

"Please be reminded Chief Inspector that the coroners verdict was misadventure, that the deaths of those men was not unlawful. You cannot overturn a coroner's verdict without an appeal to the Attorney General and if my recollections are right, it is a long and tortuous process.

Saxby grinned, " I have no interest in overturning the inquiry's verdict. 'Misadventure' does not exclude a criminal activity and the Crown Prosecution Service agrees with me. So, I ask again Mr. Lincoln, are you prepared to cooperate."

He was somewhat thrown by the statement but leaned back and simply stared at Saxby.

Saxby sighed and flipped over another sheet of paper in his bundle."

"Edmund Lincoln I am charging..."

He suddenly felt a wave of fury and threw himself forward.

"You seem gleeful Inspector Saxby, a nicely wrapped up case so you think. You have the audacity to act as though I've committed some heinous crime. Where were your bloody people when my shop was raided? Four successful hits in two years, almost eighty five thousand pounds worth of stock stolen – eight people and their families facing the loss of their livelihood and possible destitution, Add to that a huge problem in trying to restore everything. And what did the police do? I'll tell you, fuck all! We were left with no one prepared to insure us or defend us – a bloody dangerous situation. So what were we to do? Admit it – we did you and your lot a favour – those men were probably responsible for a large number of unsolved crimes in this country. Now you can rest easy because of what happened.

Do I hear any thanks from you Inspector Saxby? No tributes from our wonderful law enforcement organization? Oh no? Seems you only go for the victims and not the criminals – and why not, they are nice easy targets aren't they. You should be bloody ashamed of yourself; I strongly suggest you rethink your priorities because at the moment they are patently askew. Nothing to say? Well then, do as you will. I'll fight you every inch of the way."

Saxby perceptibly sank back as the tirade continued and only straightened as it finished. He said nothing but looked at his notes again.

"Edmund Lincoln I am charging you under section 31 of the Offences Against the Persons Act of 1861. You will stand before the magistrates for committal within the next 48 hours. Until then I am agreeing to bail. Your solicitor will explain the details."

He turned and made a sign to Compton who leaned forward and switched off the recorder, at the same time withdrawing the cassette.

With that Saxby and Compton silently left the room leaving him with Greenway who, like them, remained silent as they departed.

"Offences Under the Persons – what? What the hell is that?" he asked Greenway.

Greenway looked amazed.

"Dear God, I haven't heard of that since my days in training. If I remember correctly that are charging you under the old...well, the revised mantrap laws. It's an act legislated back in the 1820's to prohibit the setting of spring guns, mantraps and other machines calculated to destroy human life or inflict grievous bodily harm. I can't ever remember a case involving it – not in the last hundred years that is."

It was a distinct blow. Nailing him under an antiquated law, which had so it would seem, hardly surfaced in over a century was astounding – surely not!

"So what do we do now – bow our heads?"

Greenway gave a flick of his head. "Lord no – we wait for Nathan Elliot to get here and we start calculating – about how stupid the CPS have been! We've got 48 hours. I think the strategy meeting with Mr. Elliot can take place before the magistrates hear the case. Let's see what Mr. Elliot has to say. "

21

Nathan Elliot sat in Greenway's office half listening to Greenway and reading the preliminary brief with a bemused expression on his face.

He sat bemused too, silently watching both his legal advisors, and wondering how it was they could treat their client's woes with such casualness. So far Elliot had hardly offered anything that might be optimistic or encouraging. He had hardly reacted when he was advised of what charges were pending, not even expressing surprise. After about thirty minutes of briefing, Elliot sat in self-contemplation, while he and Greenway watched the old legal warrior cogitate on the case notes and brief papers. Then he turned to the both of them.

"What makes this case particularly troublesome is that the men who raided you shop are dead. Under the Act under which you are charged the equivalent level of seriousness would be manslaughter or murder. The former most likely, because it is probable that we can show it was not premeditated. However, the law applies whether death occurred during an act of burglary or not. As I recall, the act was introduced to protect the innocent from being crippled or killed by mantraps. Now, I do believe you will be committed for trial tomorrow and that being so we must ensure you are granted bail. I believe we can get that concession. As for the trial, you could of course plead guilty. With the exception of yourself, that would make everyone - including the CPS I might add – breath a sigh of relief. With the right pleading and a sympathetic judge, I suspect a guilty plea would result in a nominal custodial sentence – say a year to eighteen months. If, however, you decide to fight we will have to use the persuasive and credible arguments that the men who died were criminals – all of whom were in the process of a criminal act – and were therefore at risk of whatever befalls someone taking part in a criminal act. It is in no way specious to submit that particular claim and, should we get a sensible jury, I suspect they will agree with that contention. I propose we decide fully on our approach and strategy when I have had the chance to ponder on this a little more. In the mean time, I want to know as much about the background to this as possible Mr. Lincoln. I stress, as much as possible! I will liase with Mr. Greenway and he will convey any queries I have after your committal. We will of course meet again before your trial and I will be able to give you more considered and representative advice by then. Now – any questions? No? That's good. I'm due in court this afternoon and must be on my way.

Oh! One last thing, I know how you feel Mr. Lincoln but you are not to vent your spleen to the newspapers. Better we keep ourselves to ourselves for now. If the press wishes to speculate, or campaign on your behalf, all well and good but we are not to provide ammunition for any particular point of view. Let matters transpire as they will."

Elliot stood up, folded his glasses and shook hands. He was in conversation with Greenway as the solicitor took him to the door and in a short time was gone.

When Greenway came back he ignored his re-appearance and remained seated, feeling much less optimistic than before. Perhaps his demeanour prompted a reassurance from Greenway who looked at him over his heavy black-framed glasses.

"I take you are unhappy with what Nathan Elliot said."

"How else should I feel – the best he could offer was twelve months in jail."

"He told you as he saw it – he's not going to lie or attempt to make it seem a walk in the park. You are facing a serious charge and regardless of public opinion the courts will apply the law. The law you understand, not what the average man would call justice."

He laughed, a dry derisive laugh that expressed his whole feeling towards the law.

"Yes, the law has nothing to do with justice and don't I know it. Well, we will see – and I tell you Mr. Greenway should I get the opportunity in court I'm going to give those bastards a full layman's opinion about the law, whatever the cost."

Greenway looked momentarily shaken, and then smiled.

He fled Greenway's office at a pace, intent on finding Mark Stapleford. Driving hurriedly to the shop he reflected on the fact that there had been no sign of Mark since the arrest, and he had to know how things were. That Mark had avoided colliding with the man from the forensic laboratory in his workshop was tantamount to a miracle. An even bigger one was that so far Mark had avoided being confined to a police cell!

So long as there was nothing connected to Mark, or the rest of the staff, which was waiting in the wings to ambush him, he at least knew who the enemy was and could plan for the oncoming battle.

His car wheels kicked up odd bits of gravel as he raced down the lane at the rear of the shop and skidded to a stop. As he got out of the car he saw that the security door was pulled back against the wall and wide open. He was intent on identifying whom to reprimand for the carelessness when Mark Stapleford appeared standing at the threshold of the door.

Marks face instantly showed surprise and pleasure and he half ran forward to shorten the distance between them.

"Christ, good to see you Eddy."

"You too Mark, what's the situation?"

Mark gave a drawn smile.

"Apart from you being absent all is...well, normal. Everyone is a bit tense of course and we've had the odd invasion by the press and media but otherwise we carry on as usual. I assume you've had your anxious moments too, I'm sorry I haven't been there to back you but...well, you told me not to."

"Not to, that's right - and I'm bloody glad you stuck to it. I want no one else involved if it can be helped. On that matter how difficult has it been for you and everyone else? Has Saxby and his crew been near you? "

Mark shrugged. "Oh yes, we got the usual warning that we were about to be arrested if we didn't cooperate but no one said a word – refused to in fact. I told him that we had no intention of making it easy for him to unjustly harm someone we thought was one of the most decent people we had known, so he could sod off."

He blushed – it wasn't embarrassment, it was from a deep sense of appreciation and gratitude that he could be thought of that way.

"Well...thanks to all Mark, especially you. Come to that, how on earth did you manage to avoid that forensic guy that searched your workshop the other day and discovered the signal boards?"

Mark gave a huge grin.

"I didn't – I was in the toilet, caught short just prior to disabling the electronics. I heard voices coming from the shop I didn't recognise, talking in a tone I didn't like, so I decided I was safe where I was. I came out after you had all gone. Since then I've been managing the business as best I can. Strange to relate, sales are sky high – no such thing as bad publicity it seems."

He gave Mark a gentle slap on the shoulder.

"Well that was a bit of luck – I had fears you'd gone on the run and would eventually get sucked up by Saxby's Gestapo like vacuum cleaner. As I told you, the more you keep your distance on this matter the better."

"No fears," Mark said, "I understand from one newspaper report that the CPS are reluctant to make more of this than necessary – they don't want a repeat of last time. It's appears you are the one and only example they want, and even then they would like to wash their hands of it if they could."

He nodded – it was a reason to be cheerful.

"Okay, I'm going to make myself scarce Mark. I'm in court tomorrow and everything follows on from that, I've seen the lawyers and I'm hopeful I'll get bail again. Say hello to everyone for me – with luck I'll be back in the office the day after tomorrow."

He shook hands with Mark, and could have sworn he saw a teardrop in his eye.

22

It was a different atmosphere this time.

For one thing he wasn't an observer; this time he was the one standing before the magistrate. Nor was it as noisy and threatening compared to when Mark, Sam and Peter were arraigned. Instead there was a tension that pervaded the whole gathering, most of whom were either press or budding lawyers. It was a rare case and although he had received a good deal of press support in the short time the matter had come to public notice, there were dissenters – voices that argued strongly for 'due process'. Well, due process he was going to give them even if it killed him. He wanted his day in court – he had a lot to say, and he wanted the right platform for his critical address.

As the charge was read out and he was asked how he would plead, he replied "Not guilty" as strongly as possible. The single magistrate, this time a new stipend lawyer, brought the legal clerk forward to confer – no doubt they were as perplexed by the charge as most present, having never heard the like of it before. Once the magistrate was satisfied he found himself subject to a short address from the bench and perfunctorily committed to the next session of Crown court. At this point Greenway called the magistrate's attention to the fact that the accused was of impeccable character and the magistrate could do no harm to the public interest by allowing bail. In short, his client's record testified to the fact that he was a model citizen and would be a danger to no one. Greenway's pleading carried on and was not only well over the top but logically flawed, but it had the appropriate affect on the magistrate.

Bail was granted with a surety of £5,000 which was received by the courthouse with an 'ah!' and the odd cheer."

Thirty-five minutes after arriving in the court he was outside and free again. He shook hands with umpteen strangers, refused interviews and questions from the press and TV and finally escaped after fighting his way to the car park. Greenway was delighted but stayed with him only long enough to remind him that the date for the Crown court appearance would be in the post, a second copy being sent to his office, and that he would let him know the instant it arrived. In the meantime he had to be ready for any queries Elliot might want answering, so 'don't get lost'.

He gave a wave to Greenway as he left and felt a need to be home and away from all the turmoil. He wanted isolation and a nice big mug of coffee; more importantly he wanted the time to arrange his thinking. There was a lot to think about, not least how he was to deliver his anger and protest at the system; to expose the glaring anomalies and inconsistencies. He had already resigned himself to the consequences of infuriating the lawyers and the purists so there was no need to understate or soften his objections. He had every intention of giving vent to his feelings and he wasn't going to mince his words.

The date for the hearing was confirmed by Greenway's office a few days later. It was Winchester again and six weeks hence. At least he might get a chance to see Edward 1's mock Arthurian round table in the castle this time – he'd missed it on every visit before. Never once when he had been married to Carol had they thought about seeing it – now he had a feeling that with the aura of ancient justice surrounding the table, some might rub off on him.

His return to the shop was tinged with a degree of gloom; everything followed the usual routine but enveloped in a kind of tense expectation. He knew why and it made him feel out of place. Not only was the tension centred on him – he knew that with no insurance protection they were severely vulnerable. Furthermore, reconstructing the audio deterrent would, in the circumstances, be foolhardy. Making another system could only lead to more troubles.

He looked hard at all the risks they were facing and decided to postpone Mark's launch of their own branded Hi-Fi amplifiers. One of the reasons for this being the huge legal bills they were facing. These were potentially so draining of the business's reserves that he was resigned to having to take out a second mortgage on his house. The £12,000 he'd promised Mark for his amplifier development was in the circumstances an imprudent generosity and if cancelled could easily be reinstated once things were back to normal. There was also the problem of insurance. Its absence hung over them like the sword of Damocles; without it there was the risk of a disaster that could finish them off once and for all.

The only solution was to revisit the idea of obtaining at least some, albeit minimal, insurance cover. A futile exercise perhaps, but one he intended to pursue.

As he began to consider which of his 'to do' items had priority, his phone rang.

He blew out an exasperated exhalation – there was always someone from the media or press trying to get him to say something 'sensational' and it was odds on that this was going to be yet another.

"Hello."

"Good morning Mr. Lincoln – I'm Susanne Bryant at ITV Studio Productions – I wonder…"

"Miss Bryant I have no intention of engaging with the media. I'm sorry but…"

"Twenty five thousand pounds Mr. Lincoln – for one appearance."

"Say again?"

"We are prepared to pay you a fee of twenty five thousand pounds for a ten minute exclusive appearance on the programme 'Public Scrutiny'. We want to look at the anomalous aspects of our current legal system and it occurred to us that it was the ideal platform for you to show everyone just how bad it is."

Twenty five thousand pounds! It was enormously tempting and would make his war chest that much more resilient when it came to meeting all the costs.

"Miss Bryant, what will you want me to do – I mean, is it one to one, face to face, or will it be otherwise?"

"Well, if you haven't seen one of our programmes before it usually takes the form of three guests, all of whom have a strong opinion about something. The interviewer usually plays the devil's advocate when facing each of the guests. Everyone gets their chance to present their view but obviously their view will be scrutinised and criticised. How do you feel about it?"

"Okay in principle. I may come back to you and ask for certain assurances, please remember I am facing trial and I don't want to compromise that."

He heard a low laugh at the end of the phone.

"No, that's understood. I'll get a short form contract sent to you this p.m. We are hoping to go on air live in three weeks time. I trust you are free around that time?"

He checked.

"Nothing in my diary – no problem."

Again, a girlish laugh, "Good – I look forward to meeting you. Goodbye."

As he replaced the telephone receiver it occurred to him that he had made his bed – now he had to lie in it. Still, twenty-five thousand pounds was a welcome safety net and a damn sight more attractive than a second mortgage.

With little else to do, except jot down the odd thought about his TV appearance, he started looking for insurance brokers, those who had access to cover not usually available to conventional agents, and began phoning.

It wasn't until he spoke to a broker involved with Lloyds underwriters that he started to feel he was winning. After a discussion with the brokers he received a call from a company called *Norsted Assurance* who usually insured industrial and manufacturing sites. To his surprise they offered the cover he needed, but on condition they could use his name in an advertisement for their insurance products. It would appear in trade magazines. When he asked how it might be done he was told that they had in mind an advertising slogan along the lines of 'Whatever you are, whatever your trade, no matter the risk – *Norsted* will cover you – even if your name is Mr. Lincoln.' They wanted a picture of him but he said 'no' but they could use a picture of his shop. He refused anything else and in the end they conceded. It was no loss, the advertisement would not be released until after the trial and as far as he could see it would be a definite promotion of the business.

23

The weeks had passed uneventfully – he had a preliminary meeting with Greenway and Elliot, passed the time with the trade 'reps' representing his favourite products, each of whom always threw in a free lunch, and gave Mark the bad news about the launch of the new S&L amplifiers. Mark simply nodded his acceptance, remarking that with luck the postponement would not be for too long.

On the evening he was due be on the TV to take part in the 'Public Scrutiny' programme he was travelling through the last part of his journey by London underground on his way to the studios.

He saw an abandoned newspaper on a seat opposite and on casually scanning it he caught sight of the editorial section. It deplored the fact that he was to be allowed time on air to press his case. It argued that he was in affect to be tried by television and it could influence anyone likely to be on a jury at his trial. This comment gave him a chance to reflect on his attitude to the programme. He decided that he was going to be very guarded, cautious or circumspect in his comments, irrespective of what was thrown at him. It was no advantage to disgorge his views prior to the trial – it would arm the opposition and leave him vulnerable.

On arrival at the studios, he was received courteously by a very attractive women who's voice he had come to recognise. She showed every sign of being sympathetic to his situation and was at pains to assure him that it was not the intention of the programme to embarrass him.

As it turned out she was right – he was the least battered of the three guests sitting in front of the interviewer, a well-known face on television; one Thomas Brewer.

The guests sat in a semi-circle around Brewer with himself flanked by the other two guests and all three equidistant from the Brewer. It was far from intimidating – as the auditorium lights brightened he'd found himself looking out at a semi-circle of faces making up a small but select studio audience. As he was introduced, their applause was resounding.

Brewer was very sharp and insightful and gave the two men on each side, a tutor in law at Oxford, the other a practising barrister, a hard time.

He began by asking them why it was that regardless of the iniquities and anomalies thrown up by the law as it stood, the legal profession and those with influence made no immediate effort to have a bad law changed, retracted or amended by parliament. Was it, he queried, because the legal profession made more money the more complex and baffling the intricacies of a law or statute were, or was it that appeals against judgements made under a bad law made even more money.

He remembered the sense of outrage each of his companions expressed – blustering their way into counter arguments but finding it hard against Brewers determination to meet each protest by citing various iniquitous cases that had created a public scandal.

When at last he was introduced to the audience, Brewer gave a very brief overview of the history behind his appearance. There was no doubt Brewer knew enough detail to treat the whole thing sympathetically.

"Mr. Lincoln, what say you about the law? Three of your staff go on trial accused of manslaughter when it is obvious to all that they are physically defending themselves against a malicious, not to say vicious, adversary. Then, because criminals have nearly destroyed your business you have to resort to an active, and lethal, anti-intruder system because you can no longer get insurance to protect your shop, stock and people. You too are now facing trial for the deaths of four, maybe five, criminals who intended to pillage your shop. Don't you think that the way the law works is crazy?"

He gave the query a diplomatic answer.

"Not necessarily the law per se, but certainly the blind and dogmatic process behind it is. To insist that due process is pursued even in the face of how ridiculous the procedure is, in that it will inevitably be futile, is a waste of time and public money and an embarrassment to the whole concept of justice. I believe..."

The audience had just begun to applaud when the man to his right interjected.

"The law cannot be perfect, but those behind it, and those that defend it, do so honestly. The law maintains and underpins civilised societies - lawyers are its framework

they, and the judges, seek justice!"

He turned and addressed the speaker, this time with much less restraint.

"The law and lawyers you have so high a regard for are generally reviled by most of the population. They are not impressed by subtle legal arguments when a judgement comes down which runs contrary to common sense. The average man wants to see a process that results in him being able to say 'that is just'. He should not need a ten page closely written judgement from a judge justifying a decision based on an intellectual subtlety tied to a trivial aspect of the law. No right thinking man should have to say, 'I don't think that is fair'. Indeed, and more to the point, one should not have to say 'how the hell did he get away with that', or 'what a stupid outcome'. May I remind you that in Holland they say that if you want black to be white, you get a lawyer."

The applause that followed was long and sustained.

Brewer held his arm up to calm the audience.

"But isn't it true that in a sense the law as set down is passive – surely it is the lawyers behind the Crown Prosecution Service that decide if it is to be applied. And therein of course is the flaw. Too often prosecutions happen when they shouldn't and don't happen when they should."

The left hand guest jumped in.

"But it must be seen in terms of whether a prosecution will succeed – and that requires someone who knows the law and what evidence there is that it has been broken. If so a trial follows. That is what the CPS do."

Brewer continued. "Any thoughts on that Mr. Lincoln?"

"Only that with so defective a system its purpose becomes inverted. Instead of dispensing justice it too often creates injustice. But that does not offend the lawyers; being able to appeal a judgement means more money for them so nothing changes. Look at the Human Rights Act – as you say, so often it helps those it shouldn't and doesn't help those it should. Anything so blatantly unjust needs revision, if not striking out."

This time he almost got a standing ovation, with many of the audience on their feet.

As the applause died down Brewer closed the programme. The guests were left on the stage while the audience filed out. As the final few from the audience vanished, Brewer turned and offered his appreciation to all of them. The two other members of the panel looked sullen and were quick to leave. He was left with Brewer – who like him was collecting his notes. Standing up and looking for a way to leave the studio Brewer came up to him.

"Don't worry, I'll show you out Mr. Lincoln. Incidentally, thank you for making the show; I imagine it wasn't an easy decision for you irrespective of the fee. If it's any consolation, I think you punched well above your weight – what you said clearly resonated with the audience. I wish you luck at the trial, I know I will be cheering for you."

Later, on his way from the studios to the Underground, he felt a warm optimism. It appeared he wasn't the only one that had a bone to pick with the way the law worked; there were legions of silent, cynical dissenters out there. He could only hope that a majority of them were called for jury service in his case.

Yes, maybe he could rely on that.

In the office the next day he looked to see what the press was saying. Most of the newspapers and magazines were congrat-ulatory on his TV appearance, though one or two maintained their position that he was going to trial with a pre-ordained verdict. Nevertheless, he was encouraged by the widespread support he was getting and started to sleep a little better. Now the impending trial did not seem to be so threatening, even though he was reconciled to the possibility that the verdict could still go against him and he might well find himself in prison. The fact that in the event he was convicted there would be an enormous public outcry made the whole thing less ominous.

He seemed to limp through the next three weeks and the trial date was slow in coming. When it did, he started to wish it hadn't. But there was no running away and he had already decided to plan for the worst.

Should he be convicted Mark was to handle the future business; everyone else was assured that no matter how bad the outcome they would not be affected. He wrote to all his suppliers outlining the situation so far, thanking them for their support and guaranteeing them a continuous outlet for their products. He checked with the bank and made payments where any debts had built up. It left the shop and the business sanitized, and able to continue without him for a while. It meant also that Mark did not have a confusing transition.

24

He got to Winchester much earlier than was necessary. It gave him a chance to be alone and able to reinforce his determination not to capitulate when the prosecution started to apply pressure. At the final meeting with Nathan Elliot he had been warned that the evidence in the prosecution disclosure was overwhelming but as Elliot saw it, it was not a question of proof that section 31 had been contravened, rather it was a question of pre-meditation on his part, and criminal risk on the part of the gang.

Now, as he stood in the cold high vaulted castle in Winchester, looking at the replica Arthurian round table fixed to the wall high above him, he took solace in the fact that it represented what he had always thought, that real justice was a perfect ideal only to be seen in a kind of utopian fairyland.

It was what one felt inside that counted, whether something was right or wrong, whether or not you had transgressed without malice or greed, whether or not those who should have defended you had abandoned you – and that when deserted by them only then did you take retribution.

He stood stock still, sucking in the righteousness of the round table's meaning and its ancient significance.

Then, spiritually well fortified he turned his back on the table and made his way to the courthouse.

It was a short walk from the castle to the courthouse but a cold wind and iron-grey skies made him shiver. As he started to climb the wide steps to reach the entrance, all sense of foreboding and dread about the case had vanished. The only thing that now disturbed his feelings were the hordes of press and media swamping the outside of the courthouse with the TV cameras using every possible vantage point to open their reports for the day's local and national bulletins.

For a moment the clamour of the waiting mob shielded him from being immediately recognised or challenged, but as he pushed his way towards the barred doors a voice shouted "Mr Lincoln – a word please."

The effect was shattering and in an instant microphones and eager faces pressed around him and he found himself unable to move.

What they were saying or asking of him didn't register, all he knew was that he was imprisoned in a solid mass of bodies and unable to reach the doors. He tried to shout a plea for them to let him through but he was being pressed into breathlessness and his voice was lost in the shouts from voices close to him. It reminded him of ravenous rats packed together, all trying to get at the one morsel of food. Suddenly the force of the crowd lifted him up and his feet lost contact with the ground. He thought he was lost.

Suddenly strong hands and arms started to pull at him and force the bodies away. He felt himself become free of the throng and was carried into the safety of the courthouse vestibule above the heads of the crowd and virtually parallel to the ground. He heard the doors slam behind him and then was dropped gently back on to his feet. As he was released and looked around him he saw three heavily built policemen. They were panting a little, and one had his helmet and uniform in disarray, but they were all smiling in triumph.

The larger of the three gave him a thumbs up, "Are you alright sir, we thought you were going to go down. We didn't think you would get out alive if you had!"

He smiled back, straightening his clothing and noting that buttons had been ripped from his topcoat.

"Yes – I'm alright I think. Thank you – all of you, I believe you are right – they're like a herd of carnivores. God that was unpleasant."

As he looked up he saw the familiar figures of Nathan Elliot and Simon Greenway, both of whom were shaking their heads in dismay.

He gave a final thankful nod to the police officers and went to meet his lawyers.

Nathan Elliot shook his hand as though congratulating him on an unexpected win on the lottery – was it that he had expected to see his fee disappearing before his eyes?

Simon Greenway also felt obliged to treat him in the same way, or so it appeared.

Elliot looked at his watch, "We're due in court in ten minutes, I need a word with you first. There are client/lawyer meeting rooms somewhere so let's grab a coffee and find a room for a quick resume of strategy."

It was a warm and cosy room, and the coffee very welcome. Elliot began the moment they were seated.

"I'm going to put you in the witness box. You know already that I had certain reservations about that because I didn't want to risk you having a battle with the prosecution. However, Jacob Parris is prosecuting and I've crossed swords with him before.

He's a pragmatist and my feeling is that the CPS have not given him free rein – if the case starts to slip he'll capitulate. I'm aware he's going to put up everyone that can make the case against you look like a premeditated killing. However, we are both aware that the evidence is dependent on the one pivotal claim, that you deliberately installed a system which you knew was lethal. Take that away and we have a very good chance of allowing the coroner's inquest verdict to support us. Now, when I, or the prosecution call you to the witness box, please, I beg you, don't lose your rag. I remember watching you on TV and I have a good idea of where you stand. Try not to allow your resentment to surface and so make you appear a vengeful and vindictive individual, otherwise the claim that the acoustic deterrent system you installed was not intended to be lethal goes out the window. And *a propo* the TV appearance, we may have a problem with the jury – Jacob Parris may have objected to some of the selection on the grounds that they will have been influenced by the programme. Anyway, we will see. Are you okay with this?"

He said 'yes' but actually was somewhat indifferent to the whole process. No matter the danger, if he got the chance he was going to say his piece and to hell with whatever it made him look like. This was an opportunity to raise two fingers to the whole bloody tribe of pedantic, inflexible and dogmatic bureaucrats who had forced this ordeal on him. He wasn't going to miss the chance.

25

He stood in an elevated dock – the accused – no, the victim a she saw it – under scrutiny by a crowd of press, public and fascinated lawyers, all hoping for a sensational outcome to an extraordinary case. God forbid, he thought, that they be disappointed, all I ask is I get the chance – I'll make the judiciary squirm.

The jury were sworn and now it was 'all stand' for the judge. The courtroom came noisily to its feet and after the red robed judge's usual courtesies to counsel he was finally seated and all the rest of the court officials found their place. Nathan Elliot sat on the left of the judges bench with two of his pupils, all gowned and bewigged; so too the prosecution, Simon Parris QC, on the right aided by a CPS paralegal. The judges red robes and wig gave the immediate impression of an old man but this judge was clearly only in his forties. Nathan had said nothing about him – perhaps that was to hide a bad reputation and prevent it instilling fear. But what did he care – good judge, bad judge – it was of no consequence either way.

The clerk to the court stood and addressed him.

Your name?

He confirmed.

The charge followed. "Edmund Lincoln, you are charged that on the 29th of December ...."

Outrageous, but he'd heard it before. Indeed, he only bristled as the clerk's final words rang out in the court.

"...that you did maliciously and with criminal intent cause the deaths of five foreign individuals by contravening section 31 of the Offences Against the People act of 1861."

How do you plead – guilty or not guilty?

Not bloody guilty!

"Not guilty."

The judge looked at Simon Parris,

"Proceed if you will Mr. Parris."

Parris slowly eased himself out of his seat and stood facing the judge, casually adjusting his black robe into a more comfortable position around his shoulders. He gave the sheath of papers in his hand another look and then allowed a finger of his free hand to attend to an itch at the side of his wig.

The judge leaned forward.

"Sometime today would be very convenient Mr. Parris!"

Parris stiffened, "My apologies my Lord, this is a very unusual case and as I am sure you are aware it constitutes a comparatively rare instance where the accused and the case against him has already created a great deal of – what shall I say – public disquiet. It is for the jury to decide whether or not that case against the accused is facile and whether or not the breach of Section 31 was premeditated or not. In order for that to be appropriately considered it is necessary for the prosecution to show that not only was Section 31 of the Offences Against the Persons Act of 1861 contravened, but that it was also criminal in its intention and calculated to do harm. Five men died my Lord, and we can show that these five men died what was probably an agonising death. These deaths were at best criminally negligent on the part of the accused or at worst calculated, deliberate and intended to do harm. By installing an intruder deterrent of such alleged lethal action the accused was, and here all other considerations must be put aside, acting unlawfully in breach of section 31 of the OAP of 1861. The jury may be aware that as it stands the charge has its equivalence in a charge of manslaughter or murder and is equally as serious. I will call witnesses to attest to the fact that the deterrent was so designed as to avoid detection and the implication of this should be obvious to any impartial observer. Add to this the fact that the accused apparently kept the system hidden and secret from his own staff lays the blame for the deaths of the five men in question firmly at the feet of the accused. Further, it is of no account as far as Section 31 is concerned that the dead men were killed in the act of committing a criminal offence – in that they had broken in to the premises jointly owned by the accused and were attempting to steal his stock. The court should be reminded that section 31 protects the guilty as well as the innocent from being injured or killed by mantraps of any kind. It was enacted primarily to protect the innocent – better one guilty man is left free from injury than an innocent man becomes unjustly and murderously trapped. On this rests the principal and the *raison detre* of the 1861 act.

My Lord, the prosecution calls as its first witness Dr. Alan Norman – senior forensic scientist at county police laboratories."

'Well,' he thought, 'so much for avoiding the idea of 'rightful defence''. Parris had really given transparency as to why the CPS had insisted on prosecution.

He watched as the familiar, and this time warmer and much healthier face of Dr. Norman appeared in the witness box and was sworn in.

Parris began his series of questions with "Dr. Norman, please tell the court what the intruder deterrent installed by the accused actually was."

Norman turned slightly and looked at him in the dock as if to reaffirm his intention to be a hostile witness.

He stared him out.

"My team ascertained that the deterrent system was based on two home built signal generators feeding a large number of extremely powerful audio amplifiers. By means of a switching system the two signals could be sent independently to all the amplifiers and/or separate loudspeakers in the shop. This produced an immensely powerful sound field made up of two frequencies – a very powerful high frequency radiation and a hugely, even more powerful, low frequency vibration. Looking at earlier data in this area, caught in the high frequency sound field you would first experience cognitive confusion, nausea, loss of focus in your vision all eventually leading to positional and functional incompetence. This would be followed almost immediately if not simultaneously by a desire to escape the effects. However, in the accused's set up the victim is also subject to the low frequency sound field that has the effect of causing your internal organs to resonate; that is to vibrate severely. Depending on your physiology, that is your body mass, height, age or health, your liver, kidneys, spleen or heart would shake violently. Any one organ rupturing would be fatal. It was just like being hit by the shock wave of a detonating bomb or an extremely powerful earthquake which is how we came to understand why the intruders died."

Parris seemed happy with the response and turned to Elliot. "Your witness."

Nathan Elliot stood staring intently at Norman. It was intended to imply he was deeply puzzled.

"Dr. Norman, pray tell the court – how did you come to establish the effects you describe?"

Norman hesitated "If I understand your question correctly,

by analogy. We had evidence of similar effects from victims of battlefield explosions, violent earthquakes and from some victims from Nagasaki and Hiroshima effected by the atomic bomb's shock wave during the Second World War."

Elliot lifted his hand to block anything further from Norman.

"Thank you Dr. Norman. So, if I am not mistaken, you never actually tested the system itself – that is, you had no direct evidence of its effect on a human being?"

Norman shook his head, "No, not directly – it was too dangerous. But that doesn't change the fact that the five victims were the guinea pigs so to speak, and they proved its lethality."

Elliot smiled; it was a good reply,

"That would be true if you knew for certain that each of the victims had, as you say, the right physical conditions to be susceptible; but can you be certain that they definitely died as a result of the sound field created by the system? After all, not having tested it you have no proof that it actually worked. Is there no other reason why the victims might have died as they did?"

Parris stood up "Objection, the witness is not a physiologist or an expert in the possible alternatives to the form of death."

The judge nodded. "You should rephrase your question Mr. Elliot"

Elliot turned and smiled up at the judge, "No further questions my Lord."

It was clear that the weight of evidence was moving the wrong way. But as he sat in the dock he felt no anxiety. Having resigned himself to the trial going against him it didn't really matter. He watched listlessly as the next witness, another familiar face, took the stand. It was Murray the pathologist and he appeared fraught. He took the oath haltingly.

Parris made his usual welcome to the witness and began.

"Dr Murray, as pathologist in this matter, did your findings concur with the statements made by Dr. Norman?"

Murray looked taken aback and mystified.

"I don't know, what did he say?"

The jury and the onlookers in the public seating laughed.

Parris appeared surprised and embarrassed, "You were not in court when Dr. Norman was giving evidence?"

"No! I'm late arriving, only just got here. I'm sorry, it was unavoidable – another suspicious death."

Parris gave a short lift of his head as though hoping for divine intervention.

"Well then, let me précis Dr Norman's remarks – the deceased men in question died though severe vibration of their internal organs, causing various organs to fatally rupture. Further, that this vibration was as the result of a very powerful sound field, emanating from the deterrent system installed by the accused. Can you confirm Dr. Murray that internal organ failure killed these men as outlined?"

Murray once again looked uncomfortable if not inconsolable. Hs speech now was terse.

"I can confirm what killed four of them in terms of pathology, I can also tell you what the fifth died from, but exactly how these deaths were contrived I can offer nothing authoritative. I'm not a physicist or an acoustics expert."

Parris looked slightly aggrieved, "But the deaths could be linked to...did you say four of them?"

"Yes, four died from haemorrhage due to ruptured livers and kidneys, the fifth died from congenital heart failure – he would have had a poor prognosis anyway. But he showed no sign of any obvious internal disruption. I made this clear in my first report and it was disclosed at the coroner's inquest."

Parris took a few seconds to compose himself.

"Let us be clear abut this Dr. Murray, four of the intruders had ruptured internal organs and it killed them. Yes?"

Murray nodded "Apparently so. I could find no other reason for their demise."

"And you have no reason to dispute the fact that they were subject to a very powerful sound field which caused the disruption of their internal organs."

Murray gave a slight shake of his head, "I can only tell you what the pathology was – I can speak of the effect but the cause is outside my expertise."

Parris looked dissatisfied but unwillingly turned to Elliot. "Your witness."

Elliot smiled a congratulatory smile at Murray – if anything this witness was going to be an ally.

"Dr. Murray, I am sure the court appreciates your reluctance to speak on matters outside your expertise. May I ask if you have ever seen a similar cause of death as far as the four men you speak of is concerned?"

Murray shook his head. "Decidedly not!"

"So as you infer, there is no sure way of determining what actually killed them, by that I mean there are no precedents you can rely on."

Murray again shook his head.

"Only that mentioned at the inquest – the similarity with explosive shock wave or earthquake victims."

"You say 'similarity' – the pathology was not identical?

Murray gave thought to the question.

"On the limited evidence I have seen, the difference was in the range of internal damage – in the case of the four men the post mortem organ disruption tended to be liver and kidneys, whereas

160

other victims on record presented a much wider range of internal damage. Not all of it from one cause."

Elliot gave the jury a knowing look.

"That being so Dr. Murray, can we say categorically that we know how the four men who died in the accused's premises that fateful night were killed?"

Murray leaned forward on the edge of the witness box and shook his head.

"No – there is in no definite way. We can speculate, and perhaps be suspicious, but without testing the accused's system on an extensive range of human subjects there is no proof."

Elliot gave Murray a courteous bow "No more questions my Lord,"

As Murray turned to leave the witness box the judge interrupted him.

"Dr. Murray, one moment please, isn't it possible to employ another animal to simulate a human target for the system – surely a pig or something would suffice?"

Murray smiled.

"Indeed my Lord, but it creates too many counter claims regarding equivalence. I am told that the acoustic profile is different, by that I mean the way the sound field envelops the target. The internal organs are not positioned the same as in a human and their weight and constitution is slightly different. In short, it might tell us something...an indication perhaps, but nothing absolute."

The judge nodded. "Thank you Dr. Murray."

Parris leaned over to Elliot and they spoke briefly. Elliot then stood up.

"My Lord, my esteemed and learned colleague Mr. Parris has deemed it unnecessary for the prosecution to continue beyond this point. I am therefore at liberty to call one further witness. I call the accused, Edmund Lincoln. "

26

He was taken aback; it was certainly not his turn – not considering the expected stream of witnesses that should have been presented. Where for instance was DCI Saxby? Not to have the investigating police officer on the witness stand was strange. Yet, he supposed that things were unfolding as they should – at least he didn't have to wait to give vent to his feelings!

Yes, he promised to tell the truth, the whole truth and nothing but the truth – and as he stood in the witness box, looking around the court at every eager face and pair of eyes focused on him, it was clear they all wanted to hear his side of the story. If that were true, so be it!

Elliot looked up at him and gave an appreciative nod.

"Mr. Lincoln, the installation of this acoustic deterrent in your premises – why was it necessary to go to such lengths?"

"My business was attacked or burgled five times in all, the business and the livelihood of myself and my employees was almost destroyed. In the end I couldn't get insurance and what with the constant drain on my finances and marketing operations, the suspension of business while we restored everything, the loss of business from cancelled orders and so on, we were ultimately facing ruin. Every break in or attack, and that includes the Dighton debacle, took us down a notch and it takes a very long time to recover. The police did nothing to stop the raids or apprehend those that had carried them out. So what do you do when the system that supposedly protects you is so indifferent to your plight that it leaves everyone with the impression that the wrongdoer, and not the victim, is better protected by the law?"

Elliot said nothing immediately, appearing to deliberate on his next question.

"You say better protected by the law – that's not true is it?"

He almost snarled. "Isn't it? Then why am I here? The state removes from the wronged individual the right of retribution in order to create order, avoid mob rule, vendettas, lynching parties and vindictive accusations. But when the state fails a wronged victim to the point of utterly abandoning them, then the victim has the right to respond. Otherwise, in effect, the state condones the wrong done to the victim."

Elliot gave his reply time to sink in. Some of the jury were now leaning forward in their seats anticipating an even more cutting protest.

"But does that give you the right to entrap wrongdoers, to the point where they are at risk of their lives."

"It wasn't intended, but what choice did we have? We had to stop any further damage to our business or go under. We had no insurance, no protection from the civil powers and because of that we were exposed and vulnerable. There was no hesitation in what we did because we had to survive – or am I to be told we should have let the business and the lives and families of all my people go to the dogs rather than hurt a nice set of bandits? Listen to me; the reptiles that broke into my business were at risk. In perpetrating a callous crime – yes callous – by wanting to satisfy their greed and contempt for honest people, by not giving a single thought about the consequences, they deserved everything they got! Make no mistake, this court should understand that what I did I would do again without compunction or a second thought."

"So...what was it you did do?"

"I installed an anti-intruder deterrent based on a powerful sound field."

Elliot nodded. "Did you test it, did you know its effect?"

"Yes – it was tested. It disabled three chickens, a sheep and a goat to prove it worked. The test demonstrated that it would do what we hoped – if, that is, we were invaded by chickens and goats!

There was laughter from the public galleries.

He paused and then continued.

"By analogy, it would impede human invaders too. I have no regrets about its installation."

"So, you have no regrets. But having broken the law, do you not think the court would approve some sign of regret, an apology?"

He bristled with the remains of the pent up fury he had been holding back.

"No – no regrets, no apology. Nothing you or this court, or the stupid bleeding hearts, who have more sympathy for the dead raiders than their victims, will make me think otherwise."

At this the court erupted, there were cheers and clapping, even some of the jury stood up and clapped. The judge called for quite but his voice was drowned out.

As Elliot paused to let the outburst settle, Parris stood up and took his attention.

As the noise slowly died down Elliot turned to the judge.

"My Lord, in the interests of justice I give the floor to Mr. Parris."

Parris approached the witness box.

"Mr. Lincoln, you make no effort to hide your disdain for the rule of law. Was it not your attitude that caused you to dismiss the consequences of installing the system that killed..."

The judge interceded. "As of this moment, Mr Parris, the court has not heard anything that proves conclusively that the deterrent system did kill the deceased. I suggest you rephrase your question."

Parris looked admonished but did not hesitate.

"Mr. Lincoln, was it not your cavalier attitude to the law that caused you to dismiss the consequences of installing a deterrent system that might have been the cause of injury to the intruders?"

"No − I used to have respect for the rule of law. As for the deterrent, it was purely self defence."

Parris leapt on the answer.

"That being so you betrayed the whole concept of the rule of law did you not? It was contempt for justice?"

The question left him fuming.

"Contempt for the rule of law? No. Contempt for its massive shortcomings, contempt for its failed efficacy, process and fairness, yes. The law as it stands is a barrier to justice. Why is the law sacrosanct? No matter that it is anomalous, ambiguous, ineffective and fundamentally unjust. The law and its enforcement failed me, and my people, more than once. It has failed many others too, yet you and your kind defend it like holy script. You dare to talk to me of justice! Let me tell you, as many will know, the law and justice are entirely different things. An analogy of the law as it stands is a diseased, inflexible, anomalous edifice, too large, too complex and too flawed to really dispense justice as the right thinking man sees it. It's revered by the judiciary who treat it as an intellectual game, revelling in its subtleties, niceties and the obscure aspects of one interpretation of a particular law or another. It has its own lexicon and language, wholly unintelligible to those outside its borders and then, when written down, not even clear to those who drafted it. The law, as

Dickens described it, is an ass."

Parris stood in shocked silence while the sound of stamping feet came from the public seating and the gallery. The judge's face had drained of blood and there was a sense of rage in the crowd.

Parris then turned to the judge for support who in a loud voice said, "You are in a privileged position while in the witness box Mr. Lincoln but I caution you to demonstrate to the jury and the court a greater respect and appreciation of the nobility of the law. Continue as you are and I will treat your remarks as contempt of court. Your record shows you were a model law-abiding citizen prior to this charge. You respected the law once, why not now. Is this not a fair trial?"

As the question was raised the clamour from the crowd fell silent.

He turned in the witness box and faced the judge, looking directly into his eyes.

"You mistake me sir – I still am law abiding. Except for trivial transgressions, like speeding fines, I have never done anything unlawful other than what I am wrongly accused of here in this court today. You speak of a fair trial – I say as many do that there was no need for a trial in the first place. Do you know what an ordeal I, and those close to me, have been put thorough to satisfy due process? I see nothing wrong in eliminating criminals who are an enemy of the people and the state. I would not take a life unless it belonged to someone that injured, hurt, exploited or ran roughshod over the weak and innocent. Criminal scum have no place in a civilised society. My deterrent was installed to prevent crime, irrespective of how it did it."

The court erupted with cheers and applause. Even the press joined in the uproar.

The judge bided his time and after Parris had give the judge 'no further questions' and had regained his seat, the court settled.

He was led back to the dock, rather pleased he had not betrayed his intention to speak his mind even though he knew it would be his undoing.

The judge turned to the jury, and as the court descended into silence he started his summing up.

"The jury will disregard the remarks and opinions expressed by the accused. They are mistaken and have no place here. We are only concerned with whether the charge brought against him has been proven beyond all reasonable doubt. If you believe it has been proven you must return a verdict of guilty. If not, then the verdict is for acquittal. Under section 31 of the Offences Against the Persons Act of 1861 the illegal act is setting a mantrap. You are not required to consider whether the accused had reasonable cause to set a mantrap and simply took action in self-defence. There is no lawful or mitigating reason under section 31 to set a mantrap – a mantrap is a mantrap and it is unlawful. Furthermore, it is of no consequence that the men who died were carrying out a criminal act. That said, I direct you to the fact that not once was evidence demonstrated that the sound system installed in the premises of the accused had definitely killed the intruders. However, since there is no other reason for their deaths, we cannot but conclude that it was the system that directly or indirectly, caused their deaths. As such, their deaths were unlawful even under other statutes, not necessarily the current one. In short, what they were doing does not excuse the use of mantraps. Indeed, the whole purpose of the 1861 act was to avoid the maiming, crippling or demise of innocent people. It was accepted that it simultaneously protected those who were not innocent, but better that than an innocent becomes a victim of a mantrap and is maimed, mutilated, crippled or killed. I tell you therefore that the deaths of the men taking part in the illegal entry into the accused's premises has no say in the present case – it is merely a consequence of an irrefutably unlawful act. You are reminded that the accused pleaded not guilty to the charges against him – and yet admitted to the installation of the deterrent sound system. It is for you to decide whether the accused views the charge against him as invalid and improper, or whether he simply views the charge as perverse and contrary to the facts – that there was never an intention to do permanent harm. Regardless of such a contention, as the facts stand, and in terms of the accused's own admission, the deterrent installation was intended to have a physical effect on intruders and this is indisputably contrary to section 31. I therefore direct you to your duty. I trust your decision is swift and focused on my remarks. The jury may proceed to its deliberations."

27

He waited with Elliot and Greenway in the court's anteroom waiting for the verdict. They had provided hot coffees and he was immensely grateful for the refreshment; not realising how dry he had become. Neither Elliot nor Greenway had much to say. It was as though they were personally offended, if not deeply embarrassed, by his outbursts in court but were reluctant to say so.

"What and where will I serve my time?" he asked Elliot.

"That's a touch pessimistic after all I have done for you."

Elliot replied, "I was watching the jury and a good many were obviously on your side. Let's wait and see – even with the judges directions insisting on a conviction we can always appeal."

Greenway looked up from his coffee. "I think it's going to go against you I'm afraid. It's indisputable that you breached section 31. The jury has no choice."

They brooded for another half hour until a court usher put his head around the door.

"The jury are filing in – you need to get back."

He was back in the dock ready for his fate, stealing himself for a prison sentence made the more punitive because of his outspoken comments, and a judge who would make him pay for them. But he'd had his say and it was clear he wasn't alone in despising the way law and order worked. There were many more, even in the courtroom, who were inclined to the same view as him.

As the jury returned to their seats the foreman, a balding man dressed in a dark blue blazer of vintage style, stayed standing.

He waited as the judge settled in to his chair and the courtroom became silent. The clerk to the court rose.

"Members of the jury, have you reached a verdict?"

The foreman replied, first with a throat-clearing cough and then "We have my Lord. We find the accused Edmund Lincoln not guilty."

The judge was the first to react; he came upright in his chair so quickly his wig slipped. Simultaneously the courtroom erupted in pandemonium, though the claps and cheers tailed off as the press scrambled to get out and phone in a report.

He remained transfixed to the floor of the dock –still trying to register the verdict in his mind and wondering if he was allowed to move.

As he stood in the dock, bewildered and yet elated Nathan Elliot came round and stood below and to the front of the dock.

"You made a little bit of history – stay there until the judge dismisses you. We'll talk afterwards."

Outside the court in the anteroom he was unable to fight off the clamour from a crowd of reporters, and anticipating the TV cameras waiting for them outside he, Elliot and Greenway found refuge again in the client/lawyer meeting room they had hidden in before.

Elliot found it hard to stop grinning while Greenway's usual appearance of a sombre and joyless man had for once changed into a cross between incredulity and astonishment.

He had to ask twice why there was so much excitement about the verdict.

Elliot's smiling face gave way to a little more seriousness.

"Well old lad, it's called jury nullification and happens once in a blue moon. The jury acquitted you even though it was clear you had contravened Section 31, and they did so regardless of the judge's directions that they should convict you. The jury knew you had broken the law but they didn't believe you should be punished for it, so they returned the 'not guilty' verdict.

It warmed his heart – fairness at last and not on the basis of law.

"But surely the CPS will appeal – they are determined to get me locked up. And what about the jury – can they get away with it?"

Greenway butted in, "*Res Judicata* Mr. Lincoln, a conviction can be overturned but not an acquittal unless resulting from a corrupt trial. You're home and free. Never thought I'd be around to see a jury nullification – it just doesn't happen! And the jury are inviolate, as implied there is a precedent in law against indicting jurors for their decisions, it's prohibited."

Both the lawyers were still beaming when they were shown a side exit from the courthouse. Slipping away from the building they skirted the main thoroughfares and split when they found themselves at the gates of the cathedral close.

"Where's you car?" he asked Greenway knowing he would be travelling back the same way.

Greenway pointed in the Wessex Hotel's direction close to the Cathedral grounds.

"We arrived together – Mr. Elliot picked me up. Where are you parked?"

"Central car park, down near the Broadway."

"Elliot expanded his arms in a gesture of openness and generosity, "Since we are all heading in the general direction of the Hotel, I suggest we prop up its bar for a while and celebrate our amazing victory. As a client Mr. Lincoln I value you greatly – as a drinking partner you may rise even further in my estimation! Shall we go?"

How could he refuse?

28

It was one hell of a party. Not one of them was sober by the time the hotel bar was closed so they booked beds for the night and bade one another a tipsy goodbye should they fail to meet up again at breakfast.

When at last he did find himself leaving the hotel and making for his car in the chill of a blustery, squally morning, he was surprised that he felt no ill effects from the previous night's celebrations. It may well have been the case that his lawyers felt otherwise; they were conspicuous by their absence at breakfast.

He found his car deserted by all the others that had surrounded him when he had first arrived. It had been a long stay in the car park and he was obliged to walk from the car park into town once more in order to find a bag full of change to pay the overlong parking fee. Finding himself opposite the Guildhall, while a friendly shopkeeper exchanged a twenty -pound note for change, he looked down the street to the middle of the Broadway and the famous statue of King Alfred. It seemed to him that the upheld sword and triumphal stance of the statute was intended for him, as though some divine influence was revealing its ability to control his fate. Indeed, as he thought about it on the way back to the car he could not dispel the thought that maybe, just maybe, he was starting to win. He'd had a rare piece of good fortune, all he wanted now was to be left in peace and to be allowed to put his life back together.

He was headline news for a while, and like before began to tire of the ceaseless requests for an interview or an exclusive feature article in some magazine. But tempting though the money was, he declined at every instance – no amount of persuasion would change his mind. However, as national and world events took the front pages of all the dailies and periodicals, his story became old news and he became less and less in demand. It was a relief to be able to leave his house without either a TV crew or a reporter waiting for him. When in the end a week went by without him being ambushed, he at last felt free of his recent history and thankfully let his thinking dwell on shop business rather than it being distracted by the media. Even his staff were tight lipped and except for the cheerful welcome he received on his return to the shop, nobody was prepared to talk about the turmoil of past events.

After three weeks of everyday activities and dogged routines had passed by, he began to think back to all the plans that he and Mark had formulated before the various upheavals had scuppered them. It was time to reinstate the original ideas and to get things moving again. He'd managed to get some insurance cover at a reasonable price even though it was limited to the bare essentials. Still, it was better than nothing!

He decided to call in to the workshop.

"Mark, give me a few minutes please – bring your coffee, I'm going to have one."

Mark came through the office door, his face breaking into a tight smile. "You can't believe how much pleasure I get from coming in here knowing that the proverbial Sword of Damocles isn't hanging over us any more – it's as though the last year never happened."

A tired looking Mark sat down, caressing his mug of coffee like a long lost puppy.

He returned his partner's enigmatic smile. "Yes, I can imagine it was tough for everyone in their own way. We each have been on the wrong end of some pretty worrying stuff – we'll try not to repeat it. All things considered Mark you're due for some leave."

Mark nodded in agreement his face apparently reflecting the seriousness of the past weeks.

"I've looked at the figures Mark, and what with one thing and another, the one thing being our legal and incidental costs, the other being restoring the shop and its contents, we have moved from being very solvent to being marginally close to a financial tightrope. Now it's not that bad, we're not completely insolvent just yet and I intend to put the money I got for the TV appearance into the kitty, but I want to find a way of upping our sales a bit, that's shop retail and internet, and expanding our product range. You know I agreed you £12,000 for the new L&S amplifier development costs...well that money you will still get. But the new premises I was chasing before the crises we've just been though will have to be put aside for now. When things pick up we'll look at it again, but for the moment it's on the back burner."

He didn't think Mark would object so, as usual, a silent consent was expected. However, Mark stayed quiet for far longer than was comfortable. He stayed slouched in his chair looking unreceptive and still cradling his coffee mug.

"Got a problem with that Mark?"

Mark lifted his head and came upright in his chair.

"No not a problem but, what shall I call it, an unusual commission – a project, has appeared?"

It was an intriguing reply.

"Oh yeah? What kind of commission – one of your bespoke audio systems?"

"No – a deterrent system – just like the one we fitted here in the shop."

That came so far from out of field that he was momentarily speechless. Surely a joke!

"Come on Mark – someone's playing silly buggers. Whoever it was is trying to sucker us – it's a sting – probably the bloody press looking for a sensational story. I can see the headlines, 'No Sound Barrier for the Lawbreaker' or 'Money Not Lives For The Sound Man'. Oh yeah1 I can see it now; we're not fools and..."

Mark waggled his coffee mug trying to shut him up and when he realised Mark was looking very serious he stopped in mid sentence.

"No – this enquiry is genuine Eddy, I checked and checked again. Okay, for the sake of anonymity I only got the man's mobile number at first, but when I told him that unless I knew who I was negotiating with any discussion was pointless, he agreed a meeting with me. His name is Rafael Barrios and he's the attaché in the Guatemalan embassy in London. With so much intrigue in South America, and too many hostile neighbours for so small a nation, they want to ensure that their security is as good as it can be. They think an acoustic deterrent is just what they want, one in London and one in Guatemala City. I too had my reservations until he offered one million US dollars for the two installations."

It hit like a mortar bomb – one million US dollars!

Hr sat looking at Mark as incredulously as he was looking at him.

"Talk about a big carrot – but it's still illegal, we would be back in court before we could take breath. You can guarantee that what we were doing would leak out and the CPS would salivate with the thought of hitting us with a section 31 again. They would love a re-run of the last time they got egg on their faces."

Mark held his smile – a cheerful and knowing smile.

"Not so! I had a word with Mr Greenway yesterday. Setting a mantrap is illegal in the UK but making one simply isn't. Furthermore, every foreign embassy in the UK is sovereign territory, inside an embassy UK laws don't apply – only the embassy's own. We can't be charged with breaking somebody else's laws, or of breaking UK laws in a foreign country 'cos there aren't any. Once we are invited in to a foreign jurisdiction we are not bound by section 31. Do you see?"

He did, and it was hard to grasp. Was this the deliverance he had always hoped for? Was this the opportunity of a lifetime – some piece of serendipity that was simply too good to pass over. On all aspects it was virtually foolproof – all it needed was tight confidentiality and a good organisation.

"So, you build the system to their specification but you also have to install it, and I can't imagine any of our people wanting to fly over to some God forsaken spot and…"

Mark shook his head.

"At a million dollars a shot we can afford big bonuses. Our boys will jump at it given the amount they spend on their girlfriends and mortgage needs. As we expand, and expand we could, I'll hire another team – it's be one team on, the other off. I've got some figures in the workshop, which I'm just finalising. Give them a good look Eddy, but I can tell you now that with a typical commission of a million or more we will be somewhere close to seven hundred thousand in profit on every installation. It's far too tempting to miss – we'd be fools not to grab it."

He gave it three milliseconds.

"Damn right!" was all he could say.

29

As he surveyed the fifteen acres of woodland and formal gardens of his new house, all Lutyens in style and three million pounds worth of bricks and mortar, his only abiding regret – and still a source of emotional emptiness – was that his beloved wife Carol was not to enjoy what he now possessed. Even she would have marvelled at how easy it had been.

The day he and Mark had embarked on the new L&S business of manufacturing and installing the intruder deterrent systems had been a red-letter day. At first there was a sense of anxiety as Mark and his team had flown off to begin the first expedition into foreign territory, all carrying the concern that they could be at the mercy of both the UK's and any unscrupulous foreign authority.

But it had all gone smoothly, even with the teams arriving at innumerable foreign embassies in London, their activities had so far attracted no apparent interest from the UK authorities.

The Guatemalans had been the first to install a combined system in their UK and US embassies as well as at home. They were in no way fazed by the fact that it was likely to be lethal to any intruder. Payment had been swift – and soon they wanted a repeat of the installations at three other embassies. In order to ensure there was no delay to their commissions they had paid up-front after the initial systems were installed. They, it seemed, were delighted with the results.

They had hardly completed the last Guatemalan order when three other contacts came in. One wanted the high frequency part only to ensure that intruders would become nauseated and swiftly incompetent when exposed to the sound field. In general however, the new clients had no qualms about lethality, most insisting that the highest possible security be vested in, and by, the system. It was a foretaste of things to come and it was thought best to set up an entirely legal business operation to meet all UK business regulations and tax status. They had no intention of risking accusations of illegal trading even though technically they were not manufacturing anything. They set up *Sonic Innovations*, a subsidiary of *Lincoln and Stapleford* and ostensibly intended as a specialised arm to support Mark's amplifier development.

About how it was that one discreet telephone number gave the firm access to so much business remained a mystery, but it was clear that news about the recent trial had travelled nationally and internationally, and soon *Sonic* was being inundated. Before long Mark was hiring electronics engineers to make up a third team; but even then it was clear that even three teams would not be able cope with the additional workload. Instead of one team building systems and two carrying out installations they hired a new factory unit and took on three more engineers dedicated to the manufacture of the systems; thereby allowing three teams to be constantly on installations. Even a pair of structural engineers were on board, ensuring that the fabric of every site having an installation was capable of standing the acoustic assault. It was to ensure that the walls and ceilings would not collapse if, or when, the system triggered. Every one on the deterrent side of the business was paid handsomely and those still in the old high street shop were periodically rewarded with ridiculously generous bonuses. It made no difference whether the shop ran profitably or not, the massive income from the 'other' business easily carried it, and eventually the shop simply became a business 'front'.

Now, eighteen months into the deterrent start-up, Mark was still doing what Mark always did, pottering around with a soldering iron and a test meter, designing, and now genuinely manufacturing, a second generation of top of the range L&S Hi-Fi amplifiers. His first model had received widespread commendations in all the technical and audio magazines. If anything, Mark was more proud and more buoyant from his new found status as the designer of a widely praised and respected amplifier, than he was from the size of his bank account. It appeared that he had reached his professional zenith and the acclaim he received was nurture to his soul, it was the recognition he had always sought and hoped for. Indeed, the esteem and reputation he'd received outweighed everything else.

While he and Mark were equally wealthy, Mark sank into indifference as to how that wealth had come about or had been accumulated. Indeed, when he and Mark were together Mark would refrain from any discussion about the deterrent system, preferring to answer any mention of it with an 'everything is under control'.

It was natural he supposed. Mark wanted nothing to corrupt or tarnish his hard won reputation as a first class audio design engineer – if the source of his wealth had been openly revealed as resulting from the a lethal anti-intruder deterrent, his shining reputation would collapse.

He refrained from pressing Mark too hard on the subject – the less anxious his partner was the better.

It was his habit now to visit the shop on a Tuesday and Friday morning to tidy up any mail or sign cheques or documents. The old crowd were still there and his arrival in the office coupled to all the familiar faces; the girls in particular, arriving with his morning coffee and lingering for a chat, was a comforting routine. The days when he was absent from the shop tended to resurrect his fondness for the old times when they were just an audio outlet and he was working every day building the business. It sparked a sharp and distinct nostalgia.

Now, with changing circumstances he felt a slight redundancy. But he was too committed to his way of life to withdraw completely.

It was the familiar pattern, the routine that reinforced his own personal sense of security. Rich he might be, but he still had his duties and responsibilities to everyone else. Indeed, he enjoyed the thought that he expected to see all of his staff still working in the shop on his last day on earth – after all, they were all too well paid to even think about failing to turn up for the funeral!

This Friday morning was no different.

Janice had left the mail addressed to him on his desk. Five minutes after sitting down at his office desk looking at all the correspondence, documents and paperwork, he heard a soft knock on his door heralding the arrival of his coffee. It was a lovely ritual, not only was it a very welcome pick-me-up (and Janice made a very aromatic coffee) he would hear all the shop's gossip and learn more in three minutes with Janice than ever he could by other means. It was noticeable that both the admin girls, Maureen and Janice now dressed more elegantly, and even Mark's boys in the workshop had metamorphosised into decently attired young men. It seemed that the company's success had trickled down in more subtle ways than simply giving each staff member much more money and security – each of the shop floor sales team, Peter and Sam – now wore expensive suits and sported gleaming timepieces on their wrists.

It was as Janice began to tell him that she was sure Peter was planning to get married that Maureen knocked and put her head around the office door.

"Morning Mr. Lincoln. Mark, I mean Mr. Stapleford, says he is running late but would like to see you as soon as you are free."

He smiled and nodded his assent. Maureen disappeared and Janice said her goodbyes, not wanting Maureen to accuse her of currying favour.

As Janice vanished, he still carried the amusement of Marks' message – Mark knew very well that as a partner he didn't have to make appointments with him; at times he still behaved as a junior employee. Yet the courtesy hid something – Mark had something serious to say and it was implicit in his polite message.

He had just consigned half the incoming mail to the waste bin when he heard a knock on the door and Mark came in. He drank the last of his now cool coffee and pointed to the chair opposite his desk.

"All's well I presume, or is it bad news?"

Mark eased himself into the seat and presented a pensive if not brooding look. He leaned back in the chair, his whole demeanour apparently disheartened and physically drained.

"No Eddy, no crisis as regards business income but a personal one – I want to close down *Sonic Innovations.*"

It was a shock, not a massive one but a shock just the same. After all, it was Mark's expertise and hard work that had made them rich. Though it would take away their primary source of wealth, strictly speaking it was for him to decide.

"Any particular reason – after all Sonics has provided the

wherewithal to do all the other things you wanted to do. Are you sure about this?"

"I am! I've struggled with this decision for a long time now. Okay, I know we have profited massively from the deterrent business, but I no longer want to live with the thought that we make money from something that can kill people. Ever since the prototype system killed those intruders I've had to suppress an ever-growing sense of guilt. I want to free myself of the thought that I'm could be responsible for more deaths the more systems we install. It's not as if the deterrent installations are where criminals are likely to appear. Espionage isn't necessarily a criminal venue, what happens if an innocent worker gets exposed, or one of our own agents gets nailed?"

He saw Mark flinch as he expressed his fears.

"Come on Mark – it's too late in the day to start thinking that way. You can't go back and remove all the installations; they're a fact of life and will do what they do for a long time yet. Better you let your sense of guilt see a more pragmatic side – the very fact that the installations are there means they will do what they are supposed to do – that is, deter intruders. Even you would admit that the installations are unlikely to remain a shrouded secret. Anyone intending to get at what's being protected will know what kind of defences are in place. The chances of an intruder being caught in the sound field is actually extremely low – who would be that stupid?"

Mark sat contemplating his reply, his fingers intertwined and nervous.

"Okay Eddy, but I still see no reason to keep Sonics going. We're getting many fewer commissions now than we used to; taking in to account the cost and size of our installation teams and the factory overheads, pretty soon our year on year profit margins will start to shrink. If we are going to close at all, and at sometime in the near future we must, it might as well be now."

"So what do you want to do post shutdown Mark, concentrate on the audio market again?"

Mark gave a shy smile and waved a hand as if to dismiss the embarrassment.

"Yeah – why not? We can afford it, and if necessary you can have a chunk of my money back to ensure we remain solvent."

He gave Mark a long look, not wanting to dissemble about his feelings and attempt to argue him out of his opinion. He didn't really believe Mark's claim about profitability, but there was no point in forcing the issue. A half -hearted Mark was not going to run Sonics with any real enthusiasm, and it would only limp along towards disaster without his expertise and drive. There was really no option.

"Okay, wind it up. We'll take it off the company house registers and notify everyone who needs to know that it has ceased trading. Get your people together and let them have six weeks notice of close down so they can find other employment. When you give them the bad news soften it by telling them we'll arrange some severance pay when they leave. After that we'll sell the surplus equipment and give the factory back to the leaseholders. That okay?"

Mark suddenly looked abashed.

"Yes, though part of the tussle I'm having about this is that I will have to let seventeen staff go. To settle my conscience I have to discard some excellent people – it's bad either way."

"Why don't you sleep on it, there's no need for a hasty decision – after all, no one is pushing you."

Mark shook his head. "Makes no difference does it - for one reason or another Sonics must close but that said I'll come back

and confirm with you how and when. Thanks Eddy."
He watched his partner exit the office deep in thought and felt
a pang of sympathy.

Epilogue

Having dispensed with the mundane aspects of his junk mail, requests for help from technically inept customers, pleas for recommendations as to the ultimate Hi-Fi system from people who disagreed with a HI-Fi magazine's opinion, cheques for parts, stock and replacements, letters from manufacturers hoping for prime positions and promotions of their products (he always refused unless it was his decision) and signing off wages and bonuses, he started to feel that he was nearing the end of his morning's grind. Lunchtime was approaching and his half-day was soon to end. He was looking forward to a light lunch and then later an afternoon in the Badminton court with an old pal. As he started to tidy his desk there was a knock on his door and Maureen came in.

"Mr. Lincoln, there is a... a policeman to see you."

He was puzzled but nodded to Maureen, "Show him in."

As Maureen opened the door to leave, a tallish figure carrying a thin document case walked around her at the entrance and stood still, as if waiting respectfully to be invited into the office further.

He instantly recognised the newcomer.

"Well, Detective Chief Inspector Saxby as I live and breath, it must be well over fourteen months since last we, what... crossed swords? Or is that analogy just a little too inappropriate? Never mind, please sit down and tell me what new charge I'm going to face."

Saxby strode forward, sat down quickly and smiled.

"No charge of any kind, and if it is any consolation I regretted having to force you through the courts."

"It wasn't you directly Saxby, it was the bloody CPS, they wanted a show trial."

Saxby nodded, "I'm aware of the failure of the CPS to see what a farce the trial could become, though I heard later that you defended yourself extremely well, almost to the point of getting jailed for contempt of court."

"Yes I did, I had a lot to say but I seemed to be getting a lot of covert help – why were you not called?"

"Ah, well! The prosecution allowed me to absent myself, they thought it was cut and dried without me – or perhaps they intended to reduce the chances that you would get convicted. Really, I just don't know – though, as you will later read, in a sense I was on your case. It was a long and involved enquiry and what I can tell you now is that we finally identified the men who died here in your shop. The suspicion that they were all from Eastern Europe was confirmed, except for the fifth man – he wasn't. His name was Alvin McPhee, a well-known criminal and an associate of a number of previous safecracking teams. However, he was at the time of his death the liaison man between the European boys and their home grown planners. It seems that a mob here in the UK was using imported gangs to hit specific targets; taking all the swag and then exporting the gang in question back home with a fistful of money. They would arrive one day, be taken to the target and shown its location, do the job the next day and be on the ferry back to the Continent after that. The UK lot used four different Latvian, Rumanian and Bulgarian teams to avoid any MO arising or forensic trails coinciding. We could never tie them down because forensics tended to be different at each site and fingerprints, if any, were unknown to us. However, McPhee was the clue and eventually we nailed the UK mob and one of the foreign teams. The rest we will get because we know who they are and have issued international arrest warrants."

It was a fascinating story and he had to admire Saxby's determination to get at the truth.

"Congratulations Chief Inspector, what more can I say? Is this visit purely to enlighten me, or is there an ulterior motive."

Saxby wriggled slightly as though uncomfortable with what he had to say.

"It isn't often I have to say sorry, but you are entitled to an apology from me and the rest of the police force. Without your, what shall I say – transgression – we would still be stumbling around in the dark. As I mentioned, it was not for us to decide on whether you should, or should not, be prosecuted – I know you realise that. However, it happened and, as I said before, I for one regret it. We could have reported Mr. Stapleford's hand in this but the CPS were not aware of his involvement."

He gave a low but disbelieving grunt as Saxby finished and was about to ask Saxby a few searching questions when the office door suddenly opened and Mark Stapleford walked in.

Mark froze in mid stride as he espied Saxby who, seeing Mark arrive, stood up and offered his hand for a handshake. Mark came forward and took the hand but obviously with extreme reluctance.

"What's this all about Eddy?" Mark asked.

"Pull up a chair and we'll tell you." he replied, "Chief Inspector Saxby is here to make amends."

Saxby gave a good-natured shake of his head.

Mark pulled a wall parked chair to the front of the desk and sat down warily.

"It seems that we did the police a favour with the deterrent system – the crooks who died were part of a European wide conspiracy and their identity led the police to the ringleaders and the imported gangs that did the dirty work. It seems it's all wrapped up and no hard feelings."

Saxby leaned forward and offered him the document case.

"It's very unorthodox but as I implied earlier, I'm going to give you a look at an abridgment of my final report on the matter – it's for yours and Mr Stapleford's eyes only. Please return it to me after you have read it. If it's any consolation to you both, you will see that we were dealing with some pretty vicious individuals – some real shits. Getting them off the streets, and stopping almost all the major ram raid operations in the UK, was a real plus. However, you will also read that the civil police were not the only agency involved – we tripped over a security operation being run by MI6. Their interest was incidental to our enquiries, but when they learned all the background to what we were doing they were very helpful. However, the less than comforting part of this is that your operations have been under MI6 surveillance for a long time – now they want a confidential meeting with you both."

He gave Mark a worried look which was returned.

"On what basis – what do they want from us?"

Saxby gave a gesture of ignorance, "All I can tell you is that they need your help."

"Help? Okay – when?"

Saxby smiled with relief "Tomorrow, here at 10.00 a.m. if convenient."

Mark shrugged an agreement.

Okay – tomorrow it is," he said.

At the appointed hour they had coffee and biscuits brought in and then he told Maureen that the office door was closed for the rest of the morning or until he said otherwise. The MI6 man that Saxby introduced was quietly spoken and in his early forties. Well dressed, close shaven with his dark hair beginning to recede, he appeared to be very easy-going. His name was Danvers and his affability was not that of a dullard, his sharp mind belied any pretence.

"Gentlemen, I regret that your activities with regard to *Sonic Innovations* have been of interest to the UK security agencies for some time. It has been a fascinating surveillance as we logged your access to almost every embassy in the UK and so many others overseas. In fact, we began to envy Mr Stapleford's team as they scuttled from place to place, always being able to get to the inner sanctums of so many usually impregnable foreign government fortresses. It occurred to us at one time that we should shut you down, but then good sense prevailed and we realised that ultimately you could be of immense help to your own side. You see, you, or should I say Mr. Stapleford and his teams, have seen the way into the secure aspects of places we would very much like to go. In short, you can tell us things we could not ordinarily know. To confirm, I take it Mr. Stapleford you still have the plans for all the deterrent system you have installed over the last year?"

Mark hesitated, then nodded.

"Excellent, so that happily eliminates the need to shut you down – the more plans the merrier we say. Now..."

He interjected.

What's this 'shutting us down'? We operate under confidentiality agreements with foreign authorities that preclude disclosure. Not only that, we have not contravened any UK law, all our installations were on foreign territory and manufacturing the deterrents is not in itself illegal."

Danvers let the interruption hang for a short time.

"True, but you failed to get an appropriate export license – you exported material under false pretences. Calling your systems simply a sound system, or an anti-intruder system, was a touch ambiguous. Likewise, you notified the tax authorities about personal earnings but not on capital gains tax or corporation tax. You registered your subsidiary company but failed to put in correct accounts to company house. As for confidentiality agreements, I can't for one moment see you being sued for breach of any non-disclosure agreement without the plaintiffs having to disclose what it was they were contracting you for. Would be a touch embarrassing don't you think? All in all, you have a good deal hanging over you, but let us not quibble – all this can be resolved."

Danvers let his grave expression slip into a smile.

"Gentlemen, this is for your country – surely I should not have to make threats."

"You seem to be doing fairly well at the moment," Mark said.

Danvers looked at Saxby who gave a slight shake of his head and refused to comment.

"Alright, to put this in perspective, we want you to do one more thing and then you are of no further interest to us."

"Really," he said, catching Marks eye, "and what is the 'one more thing'?"

Danvers looked at Mark. "We need a way of defeating the deterrent sound field – can you do it?"

Mark looked puzzled.

"How do you mean defeat it – are you asking how to ensure it won't work, or how to survive while it is working?"

"The latter – how can an individual operate with impunity while the sound field is on?"

Mark gave a short shrug of his shoulders.

"You can't – ear-defenders might delay the effect of the high frequency side but the low frequency vibrations will penetrate anything unless you are cocooned in a vacuum. There really isn't a simple way unless..."

"Yes Mr. Stapleford –unless what?"

Mark looked as though he had received inspiration by a divine route.

"Well, the individual would have to be carrying a sound cancellation system that was as powerful in his local area as the vibrations coming from the deterrent system. That wouldn't be easy, though I suppose it could be done for just a short time. Power you see – it would all depend on the available power, and the combined weight of the amplifier, battery and speakers."

Danvers seemed delighted. "What would it take to develop what you have just said, a sound cancellation system – and how long?"

Mark said nothing for a few seconds while he thought it out.

"Six weeks, maybe more as it's refined, but no promises, its not going to be easy."

Danvers chuckled, "Splendid – here's my card, I expect to hear from you regarding the installation plans and the cancellation system in due course. Good, unless Chief Inspector Saxby has anything to add, I will wish you gentlemen an excellent morning."

The two guests stood up and shook hands with both Mark and himself. He went to the door with them and seeing Janice in the showroom asked her to show the two men out. He watched them silently filing out of the showroom doors onto the pavement and then returned to the office.

Mark sat glumly in his chair.

"Don't we get it Eddy? I came back to tell you that much against my feelings I had decided not to shut Sonics down and my good intentions as far as the staff are concerned is suddenly and unexpectedly pre-empted – I can't shut down anyway. This guy Danvers then asks me to find a way to defeat the system – all James Bond stuff."

He gave Mark a wink.

"Yeah, but your idea of using a sound cancellation system carried by the individual could work – a brilliant idea if you can get the weight down."

"Yeah, if!"

"You will, it's a technical problem – you'll love it."

"Perhaps – and yes, I've a few thoughts already."

"Good, when you think about it you will be countering bad vibrations with good vibrations – that's a plus."

Mark smiled, "Never thought the Beach Boys would get in on the act. But you know, this could turn out for the best, at least my people are safe for a while."

As he returned to his chair he patted Mark on the shoulder – whatever his partner's faults they were heavily outweighed by his pragmatism and intuition.

"Funny thing is though Mark, they threaten to prosecute us unless we help them – knowing full well that had we refused, we could never have proved that they were prepared to ignore this so called illegality on condition we found a way of defeating the sonic deterrent. It seems that when it comes to the law and ethics, everyone turns a blind eye when it's convenient – in this particular case, in the interests of national security."

Mark leaned back in his chair and stretched out his arms. "What do you think they would say if I told them the truth, that none of the currently installed systems are lethal anyway?"

He froze – staggered by the revelation.

"You mean they won't work?"

Mark grinned, "Oh, they work okay – but an intruder exposed to the combined sound field would only get a very bad case of nausea, some vomiting and severe disorientation. As a deterrent system it's excellent, as a mantrap it is very unlikely to produce long-term physiological damage. I know, I tested it, which is why you thought I looked rough before our first big commission. The absence of any complaints from our customers so far implies that not one of them has been reckless enough to test an operational system using a live subject. The embassies of course are warned of the lethal effect the deterrent poses, so they follow the activation and system shutdown procedure meticulously and by the book. They have no idea I de-rated the design before we started the installations. I'm still not convinced we should still be installing them, but now we're compromised, as we are by the SIS, it's Hobson's choice"

"So, what about the noise cancellation system – still necessary?"

"Well, yes and no. Yes to avoid our own people becoming impossibly dysfunctional doing their spying, and no in terms of it being necessary to avoid anyone's death. But just think, if we begin to roll back fitting the deterrent system installations, and start providing Danvers with some very expensive, but entirely unnecessary acoustic armour, we could still have a nice little business."

He gave Mark's observation a few seconds thought. The irony of the situation made a mockery of all the carefully made rules they were supposed to abide by. How bloody stupid the whole thing was!

"Damned right!" was all he could say.

#0017 - 171016 - C0 - 216/140/11 - PB - DID1617822